POSTCARDS FROM THE FUTURE

A Triptych on Humanity's End

Novellas by

ANDREW CHARLES LARK

DONALD LEVIN

WENDY SURA THOMSON

These are works of fiction. All of the characters, establishments, events, locales, and organizations portrayed in these works are either products of the authors' imaginations or are used fictitiously and are not construed as real. Any similarity to real persons, living or dead, is coincidental and not intended by the authors.

Copyright © 2019 Whistlebox Press and Quitt and Quinn, Publishers
All rights reserved.
ISBN: 978-1-7328489-2-4
Published by Quitt and Quinn, Publishers, in conjunction with
Whistlebox Press
Michigan

ACKNOWLEDGMENTS

Andrew Lark:

It took the time and talent of many people to help create these three works of fiction that you now hold in your hands, and I would like to thank the following people for their many and valuable contributions: Bailey Kay Lockwood for the first-rate editing, and Virginia Lark-Moyer for her suggestions and feedback, and her enthusiasm for *Pollen*. A big, giant kiss of a thank you to Karen Lark for… well, for everything under the sun and more! Thanks to Boyd Craven for his thoughtful words on the stories in this anthology. Lastly this project would never have gotten off the ground were it not for the brilliant participation of Wendy Sura Thomson and Donald Levin. I got the idea for this anthology after listening to a really depressing segment on NPR about the incredible number of species that have gone extinct due to human activity. I found that news so distressing that I had to pull off the road. A thought then popped into my head: *what if the tables were turned and it was we humans who faced imminent extinction*? It was then that my ideas for *Pollen* began to form, but then I thought that this one story would not be enough. What if I were able to get two other accomplished authors on board to write their own takes on the end of humanity? Two phone calls, two "count me ins" and we were off and running, so… the biggest thank you I can possibly muster to Wendy Sura Thomson and Donald Levin. It was the pleasure of a lifetime to work with both of you on Postcards from the Future!

Donald Levin:

I wish to thank Andrew Lark for providing the impetus for this project and inviting me into it. My deep appreciation goes to my partners-in-apocalypse Wendy Thomson and Andrew for being ideal colleagues, collaborators, and editors; working with you both made contemplating the end of the world a pleasure. Thanks go to Bailey Kay Lockwood for her editing expertise, and to Boyd Craven for his generosity in contributing the introduction to this volume. Thanks also to Dave Plopa for my author's photograph, and to Joan Young for advice on the effects of long-distance hiking. My appreciation to the Berkley Public Library, where I wrote and edited much of this project. My gratitude to Paddy Lynch for the use of the Kresge Mansion for our book launch celebration. My warm thanks to Suzanne Allen for the photo on the cover page of "The Bright and Darkened Lands of the Earth," and for her keen reading insights as well as her constant love and support. For environmental information in my novella, I am indebted to: UN Environment (2019). Global Environment Outlook-GEO 6: Healthy Planet, Healthy People. Nairobi. DOI 10.1017/9781108627146.

Wendy Sura Thomson:
I would like to thank my fellow authors, Andrew and Don, for their sharp wit, sharp pencils, and sharp intellects. My involvement would not have happened without them. I also join my fellow authors in thanking Bailey Kay Lockwood for her outstanding efforts. Finally, I would like to thank my sons and daughters-in-law, Chris (Corina) and Kevin (Nicole) for their unending support and encouragement.

If you enjoyed reading this book, please consider posting a review on Amazon, Goodreads, and/or the individual author's websites.

INTRODUCTION
by Boyd Craven

What is it about Post-Apocalyptic and Dystopian fiction that seems to catch your fancy? I know the answer for me is that even though everything might go horribly wrong in the world, there's always a silver lining somewhere. Not every story has a happy ending, not every story arc can be seen to completion, just as in real life. But without being in personal danger, the reader can see and experience the struggles of the characters.

It's these struggles that seem to draw the reader in. An internal reflection of their own struggles in real life, perhaps? The thought-provoking scenarios in this book will do more for you than that. They will force you (the reader) to think and wonder to yourself: "What if that were me?"

As a reader and writer of Post-Apocalyptic and Dystopian fiction, I was thrilled when Donald Levin asked me to read through this book in your hands, and write the introduction on behalf of all of the authors. I know you'll love *Postcards from the Future: A Triptych on Humanity's End* by Andrew Charles Lark, Donald Levin, and Wendy Sura Thomson.

Boyd Craven
Best-selling author of the *Still Surviving* Series

TABLE OF CONTENTS

POLLEN

BY
ANDREW CHARLES LARK

PROLOGUE

THE CHRONICLER

I was an officer on the *USS Michigan*, a nuclear-powered submarine on the day that would come to be known as Pollen. We were on maneuvers in the Pacific Ocean off the west coast of the United States when I fell ill – grievously ill, as it turned out, so I was placed in hermetic quarantine in the submarine's medical facility and put into a chemically induced coma. I have absolutely no recollection of the days leading up to my incapacitation, but remember only waking up stewing in my own soil and filth. I quickly discovered that the mechanical diaper that was supposed to keep me clean and sanitized had clogged. It took me hours in my weakened and emaciated state, but I was finally able to extricate myself from the various IV lines, feeding tubes, ventilators, and other devices that kept me alive—for many months unattended, as it turned out—and to this day I marvel at the fact that I didn't contract a life-ending infection.

I slowly crawled out of the bed and cleaned myself. All the while I kept calling for help but no one came to my aid. I pushed the button that opened the sealed glass door and once again called out, and once again, no one came. After a while I discovered that I was completely alone on the submarine and that it had run aground. This was astounding. A professional and highly disciplined crew of naval officers and the enlisted seamen under their charge would never simply run a submarine aground then abandon ship. This just does not happen.

The mess was still stocked with food – enough for me to get by on, so I decided to remain on board. I had a nasty groin rash that needed tending to with antibiotics, and I reasoned that leaving the safety of the submarine in my state would be dangerous. *Besides,* I thought, *the crew is certain to come back.* Then I panicked, thinking that maybe the nuclear fuel had sprung a leak and the entire submarine's interior had become highly radioactive, but a Geiger counter put those fears to rest. Surely there was a damn good reason for running this multi-billion-dollar instrument of war aground. If I waited patiently, I reasoned, I'd find out soon enough, so I tended to my rash; I ate; I exercised; I rested, and slowly I got my strength back. I found the captain's log and read one vague clue to what may have happened: the submarine made an unscheduled surface on the 16th of May, 2069. This would be the captain's last entry. It was only years later that I was able to tie that fateful date to the day that would prove to be the beginning of the end of humanity – the day that Pollen infected every human being on earth, the sole exception apparently, being me.

Two months went by and I had given up any hope of rescue. I had to seriously consider leaving the safety and refuge of the submarine. This, I realized, was a great dereliction of duty, but what else could I do? By then the food stores were running low and the pumps that kept the nuclear reactor cool were beginning to show signs of fatigue; I could hear the grind of metal on metal, and they would soon fail. I had to get far away – and quickly – if I wanted to live.

I climbed out through the forward hatch and assessed the situation. She'd been scuttled into the protection of a cove, and the bow had sunk almost completely into the grey sand and stones of this cove's remote beach. Large breakers would not be a problem, but the tide could wash any supplies out to sea if I didn't carry them to higher ground, so I tied ropes to the hatch door and spent the next couple of hours shuttling things to the safety of a bluff, out of the sea's reach. I had no way of knowing exactly where I was, so between studying the topography, the captain's log, and chart entries, I surmised that we'd scuttled in a remote and unnamed cove, probably a hundred miles from the nearest inhabited area. I would have to trek southward, and do so with great haste. This was dangerous country and my place at the top of the food chain was not assured.

Eventually I found my way back to civilization but quickly determined that something horrible had happened to humanity. Information on Pollen was sketchy and vague in those early days, and legitimate news regarding the incident was soon overshadowed by conspiracy and paranoia. I laid low, kept to myself, and told no one about my inadvertent luck in quarantine on the submarine that kept me from being exposed to the slow death of Pollen. Sadly, in all the years since abandoning the submarine, I never heard from, nor saw any of my fellow crew members again; their sea-bloated corpses visit only in flashback and nightmare, tangled in kelp, and pummeled by surf.

I lived out the rest of my life in quiet anonymity and watched sadly as civilization crumbled around me. As on that submarine so many years before, scuttled on that lonely, cold, and far away cove, I left the safety and refuge of my home and traveled the vast wastes of what was once the United States of America. My ambition to find my fellow crew members never diminished, so I left many clues behind for any who may have survived – mostly slips of paper with my name and the coordinates of my home in the pages of library books about submarines.

For the sake of humankind's posterity, I collected and assembled the stories and accounts that you, dear reader, will find on the following pages of this journal. In a few, long-abandoned homes, I'd come upon valuable stories in the form of hand-written diaries. These I kept. The public archives of important and influential people, housed in the ruins of libraries and universities across this once great land, were instrumental in helping to form a picture of what had happened. These I kept as well. The decay of our once great republic is tragically evident as the realization set in for the people on these pages, and millions of others, that we would be the last generation to inhabit the earth.

I am now a very old man – exactly how old, I have no way of knowing. What I do know is that I'm only hours from drawing my last breath. If you, dear reader, have wandered into my home, then you've surely come upon this book which lies on my kitchen table. I invite you to read its contents for the stories and accountings that mark and tell the tale of the end of humanity.

Signed -
Johnathon Jerome Quinn

CHAPTER ONE – 2074 A.D.

Matthew Delvin, 53
Writer
Born: 2021
Died: 2089
Los Angeles, California

May, 2074

"It was May, 2069 - five years now, and I remember it like it was yesterday because I woke up feeling absolutely incredible, and by that I mean… euphoric. I opened my eyes and literally felt euphoric, and I can safely say that that's never happened to me before - ever. I was 48, not in very good shape, and had more than my share of the requisite aches and pains for a guy my age: throbs, creaky joints, warning signs… you know… but that morning, nothing – no pain, no anxiety, no mortal pangs.

So, I was a coffee drinker, you know? My morning routine always consisted of waking up, crawling out of bed, taking a piss, splashing some cold water on my face, then trudging to the kitchen to make a pot of coffee. I'd had this routine for years, but that's not what I did on that morning. Instead I got out of bed, opened the shades, slid open the glass door, and walked out onto the balcony, and it was… incredible, what I saw. It was early, around seven, and the sky; it was shimmering in all these iridescent colors. At first I thought it was some atmospheric phenomena - ice crystals high in the stratosphere, refracting sunlight, causing all these strange colors. Then I noticed how quiet it was. My balcony overlooks a vista of thousands of houses, a couple of freeways, skyscrapers off in the distance, you know - Los Angeles - I have incredible views, but that view comes with a price, and that's the constant din of the city below, but I'm used to it. But that morning? No din. Not a sound.

I grabbed my binoculars and looked at a ribbon of freeway and saw that every vehicle was parked. People were standing on the pavement and looking up at the sky. I mean no one was moving; everything had come to a grinding halt! I panned left toward the subdivisions and saw people standing on their driveways, and in their backyards, and everyone was looking up at the sky at all the shimmering colors. Then I looked up and it was like, I couldn't move! I just stood there… transfixed, and utterly happy, utterly euphoric.

There was a powdery element to these colors, like pollen, and that's actually the name that stuck for what happened that day: Pollen. Huge clouds of pink that would suddenly turn yellow, then ochre, and every color imaginable - it was crazy! A patchwork of iridescent colors filled the entire sky! Oh, and there was a scent too, like the air had been perfumed with the most intoxicating, most alluring scent imaginable. I lay down on the chaise and breathed in the euphoria, and marveled at all the wild colors in the sky.

I had no idea what was going on, nor did I care. I didn't do a goddamn thing that whole day. I thought I'd died and gone to heaven."

Rebecca Tindall, 20
Single Parent
Born: 2054
Died: 2089
Kearney, Nebraska

May, 2074

"I shared a bedroom with Brianna, my little sister, and I was starting to show. She had no idea that I was pregnant. Nobody did. Brianna just thought that I was gettin' fat, and she didn't hold back on the sass neither. 'You're turning into a fat pig,' she'd say, and she was right, but obviously there was nothin' I could do about it. My boobs were getting bigger, my thighs, my tummy... everything. And I had no idea how I was gonna tell mom, and that's what I'd been so stressed about. It seems so silly now, but I was sixteen, you know? And all this was before Pollen when everything was normal.

My mom, she was like super-Christian; we all were, but when I think back on it, I was probably just going along with the whole Jesus thing, I mean, I wasn't nearly as enthused about the Lord as she was. Don't get me wrong, I loved Jesus and all, but my mom? She was at a whole nuther level. She spoke in tongues and everything. She'd get super fired-up for Jesus and served as his witness like 24/7, you know, totally obsessed with saving souls for Christ. But nobody ever saw how angry she could get except me and Brianna – especially if we ever brought up our long-gone father, so we always avoided that touchy subject. Anyway, we went to church three times a week: twice on Sunday, and as mom would say, '... a booster shot of the Lord on Wednesdays.'

So it was actually on Pollen that I finally told my mom that I was pregnant. I fully expected to get thrown outta the house. I'd even packed a bag the night before just in case. But… on that morning… it was so weird. If I remember correctly, we all woke up at the same time, and I felt so happy, like all the weight and worry of the last couple of months had been lifted. And before I even got out of bed the door opens and it's mom, and she says, 'Girls, get up! You gotta see this!' And Brianna jumps out of bed all happy, and if you knew Brianna, that's not at all typical for little miss throws a hissy-fit every time you try to wake her.

So we all go outside and the air is so fresh, and there's this perfume smell, but like no perfume I've ever smelled before. And mom didn't even need to point upward. We all saw it. We looked up at the sky with all the colors shimmering as far as the eye could see. We were so happy… all of us, so I said, I just blurted out, 'Mom, I'm pregnant. I'm gonna have a baby.' And she said, 'Oh Becky, I knew. You can't hide anything from me. I was just waitin' for you to tell me. Praise the Lord, a baby!' And me, and Brianna, and mom – we just stood there on the lawn, hugging and crying tears of joy. I was so happy and relieved. Mom began praising the Lord and thanking him for all his blessings. Brianna joined in and so did I. 'Thank you, Jesus!' I kept saying. 'Thank you, Jesus!' And I meant it."

Dr. Deborah Bernstein, 48
Research Scientist
Born: 2026
Died: 2089
Chicago, Illinois

June, 2074

"I don't think there's a single person who was alive that doesn't remember Pollen. I certainly do, but unlike the hundreds of patients I've treated and interviewed since Pollen, my euphoria was peppered with panic, and I hated that I had no control over my feelings. I liken my experience to that of being under the effects of a strong hallucinogen, in that I was utterly unable to function until the euphoria had completely subsided. And since that day, it's been reliably documented that no one on Earth functioned in any way, productive or otherwise, while under the effects of Pollen. I'm still blown away by that. Think about that for a second – on Pollen there was no crime; no murders, no rapes, and no acts of larceny! Wars were not fought on that day: all commerce terminated; no one reported to work- no doctors, police, or emergency personnel; no one commuted. All traffic simply stopped!

Two years after Pollen I founded The Global Fertility and Reproduction Restoration Institute, and our mission is to restore fertility and reproduction to humankind. We're still in the early stages, and as it stands, we have more questions than answers, but even that's progress, you know? We have a long way to go and our window for success is finite, so the sense of urgency at the institute is off the charts.

We still have no idea how Pollen terminated humankind's ability to reproduce, but we're working on it; day and night, we're working on it."

Reverend Mark D. Hopper, 53
Evangelical Leader
Born: 2020
Died: 2089
Charlotte, North Carolina

July, 2074

"It's an historic day because it's the fourth anniversary of the last babies born, and I'll be speaking to the President on that very topic later this afternoon, and you know, it's still so strange and difficult for me to wrap my head around the fact that the youngest people on Earth are four years old today. Now, between you and me… I'm really struggling with this. It has me wondering if all those souls who would have otherwise been born since Pollen were in fact God's chosen, and that the rest of us have been left behind. Was Pollen God's way of calling the unborn faithful to him? Was Pollen in actuality, the second coming of Jesus? Are we truly living in the end times?

This has been the major topic of our sermons over the past year, and we're doing everything we can frankly, to keep our flocks faithful. But truth be told, all over the country we're losing thousands of congregants every month. Our nation is in a crisis of faith, and that'll be the primary topic I'll be discussing with the President."

John Radner, 22
Activist/Conspiracy Theorist
Born: 2052
Died: 2087
Kokomo, Indiana

August, 2074

"Other mammals were not affected at all! Not even the great apes—orangutans, gorillas, chimpanzees; they're reproducing just fine. Birds, reptiles, fish, insects, in fact all other living organisms came out okay. Human beings are the sole exception! Why?

This is the single-most devastating thing that's ever happened to mankind. We got about forty years, tops, to turn this around and if we fail, we'll be extinct as a species in about a hundred years.

I can't prove anything yet, but it's obvious: we've been targeted for extinction. A lot of people in my group believe this and we're gonna find out how and why the fuck this happened. You can put money on the fact that the top secret documents that outline Operation Pollen are filed away at some government facility; The Pentagon, or more probably NORAD! Shit, I wouldn't even rule out Area 51! In fact, one of our members used to be in the Air Force, and he told me that in the weeks leading up to Pollen his roommate told him that he saw convoys of tanker trucks slowly pulling into a giant hangar. Now why the fuck they got tanker trucks pulling into giant airplane hangars? I'll tell you why! You ever heard of chemtrails?"

<u>Dr. Robert Kindler, 78</u>
<u>Director, Centers for Disease Control</u>
<u>Born: 1995</u>
<u>Died: 2082</u>
<u>Atlanta, Georgia</u>

<u>August, 2074</u>

"We sent oceanographers, geologists, biologists, zoologists, meteorologists, environmentalists, marine biologists, and every other 'gist' you can think of, plus a few hundred graduate students, in the various and pertinent fields all over the world to search for samples of Pollen. We obviously have to know what we're dealing with here. We've collected and analyzed soil and rock samples from every continent, we've got tissue samples, ice cores from the Antarctic, water samples from all the oceans, seas, brackish tributaries, rivers, the Great Lakes, swamps, estuaries… you name it. Meteorologists sent balloons up and took atmospheric samples from all over the globe at various heights, and so far… nothing! Nada! Zilch! Billions of dollars spent on the search for Pollen, and so far we've got nothing – not one, single, solitary molecule of the stuff.

NASA has been floating the theory of a possible neutron star intersect, which I think is worth exploring, but it's all preliminary and Congress is screaming for results, but as usual, they're being tight with the purse strings, and yada, yada, yada! Listen, I'm not too old to bandy words over this thing: Got any goddamn ideas? We're stumped!"

Rebecca Tindall
Single Mother

September, 2074

"These days I'm not so sure about the whole 'God thing' you know? Even mom's lost her faith. She refuses to believe in a god that would allow this to happen. And I'm not that naïve, sixteen-year-old girl anymore neither. I just wish I knew then what I know now about Darcy's father, Bruce. Youth pastor, my ass.

Darcy was born around the time that everything started falling apart. Things were tough, you know? They still are. So I told 'Pastor Bruce' that he needs to help out a little, you know – financially? Step up and be a dad? And he's like, 'What are you talking about!? I'm not the father!' So, long story short, the court orders a DNA test and… here's where it gets weird. According to the results? Genetically? I'm not Darcy's mother! And Bruce is not her father; so of course he gets off scot-free and I come out looking like a whore. Whatever… I know the truth. But anyway, this whole genetic thing – how's that even possible? Of course I'm Darcy's mother! And Bruce is her father, I mean, there wasn't anybody else! And my primary concern obviously, is Darcy's health because like all the other babies born after Pollen – her ovaries are different somehow. They can't explain it."

Matthew Delvin
Writer

September, 2074

"I was exhausted afterwards. Just… you know, spent. And remember, all I did that whole day was sit out on my balcony, breathe in the scent, and stare up at the Pollen. It felt so good that it never occurred to me at the time to question what was happening. The only way I can explain my frame of mind was that I was completely in the moment. I wasn't thinking about the future, the past, or anything at all. It was the most Zen twenty-four hour period of my life.

I'd had a really successful career in the film industry in spite of some problems with addiction. And except for one fairly devastating incident, I mostly held it together, but it did get to the point where I had to check into rehab, and I came out the other side clean and sober and I'm proud to say that I've stayed that way ever since. But I'll tell you this… if I get wind of someone selling Pollen in little baggies – I'll drop everything. I'll be first in line.

Look, I know the devastation that it's caused, and I've heard all the conspiracy theories about the eventual and imminent end of mankind, which by the way is bullshit. I mean, come on! We're smart. We'll figure this out. But as selfish as this sounds… here's the deal: I'm in my fifties, and I don't know about you, but personally I wasn't planning on having any more kids anyway.

Mostly, I've had a pretty damn good life. Sure, I've made a few mistakes. Haven't we all? But if I were to wake up tomorrow morning with that familiar scent wafting in the air, and all those multi-colored clouds of Pollen billowing in the sky, I'd be the happiest man on Earth. I'd walk back out onto the balcony, lie down on the chaise, and die a happy man."

John Radner
Activist/Conspiracy Theorist

October, 2074

"And now the so-called scientists are saying that Earth may have crossed through the radiation beam of a neutron star or some shit. Yeah… that and they're actually revisiting the whole dinosaur extinction thing with this neutron star business, but we know the deal. We know exactly what the deep state is trying to do but we ain't buying it. They're just trying to bullshit us with some outer space malarkey as a deflection, you know? The problem is, is that so many people do buy into the bullshit!

I remember being taught in school that it was asteroids slamming into the Earth that caused the mass extinction of dinosaurs millions of years ago, but now they're trying to change it into some neutron star theory, like how the Earth passes through the beam of a neutron star every 65 million years or so, and that's what's caused all these massive die-offs throughout time. And now they're saying that's actually what Pollen was – a beam of radiation from a neutron star. But wouldn't that kill everything? Not just humans, but everything? I mean except cockroaches 'cause ain't nothing gonna kill them nasty little fuckers!"

Dr. Deborah Bernstein
Research Scientist

November, 2074

"A couple weeks ago we received the body of a post-Pollen female who was tragically killed in a drone accident, so naturally we performed an autopsy, and let me tell you, an opportunity like this is rare, I mean these post-Pollen children are resilient. Among the many interesting findings was that her reproductive organs were developing in ways I'd never seen before.

I'm cautiously optimistic that the post-Pollens will be capable of reproduction once they reach puberty. What's odd though is that the differences between them and us are significant – so significant, in fact, that one would be justified in saying that these kids are the next evolutionary step in human development, and this wasn't just, you know… natural selection at work. This was sudden and abrupt. These post-Pollen children, for all intents and purposes, are a different species, and that's astounding. As things are today, we're going to die off, and, provided they become capable of reproduction, they'll live on. Allow me to elaborate: as with all pre-Pollens, my ovaries, your ovaries – they've been in a gradual state of necrosis since Pollen. They've atrophied to the point where they're roughly the size of raisins. The same basic thing has happened to males and their testes; they've atrophied down to a similar size, and this has rendered both the males and females of our species sterile, and yes… we're still working on a cure that'll hopefully reverse this condition.

I don't have time for despair, but the longer I'm in this… look, I'm still optimistic, I mean I have to be, right? But I do lie awake at night and worry that we pre-Pollens have become, in a sense, modern-day Neanderthals, and I genuinely wonder… are our days numbered?"

CHAPTER TWO – 2082 A.D.

Dr. Robert Kindler, 86
Former Director of the CDC

January, 2082

"After I resigned as director of the CDC I moved back to my home in Ann Arbor. I live across the street from this old elementary school. The district closed it this year. It's no longer needed, as the youngest children have aged out and moved on to middle school. It's one of those beautiful old structures from the last century – a colonial revival. I think it's an Albert Kahn building, erected back when cities took pride in the appearance of their public structures. Anyway, it's gorgeous and a thing to behold. I used to imagine that it was the kids who kept that old building happy, like an old man bouncing grandchildren on his knee. It used to make me smile seeing that colorful jungle gym thirty feet away from those ancient, ivy-covered walls.

It's so quiet over there now, but I remember back in my writing days when it was necessary to shut the windows of my office to block the shrieks and laughter coming from the playground. I used to time my progress to the recess bells.

That old school and I have a lot in common in that we're both relics from a bygone era, and I've gotten sentimental in my old age. I actually talk to it; I told it that I splurged on something to honor our mutual obsolescence – a very old and very expensive bottle of red wine that I'm going to drink to wash down all these sleeping pills. 'To me and you, old man!'

... Goddammit, I thought we'd have this thing licked by now."

Phillip Meijerson, (Post-Pollen Juvenile), 12
Middle School Student
Born: 2070
Duluth, Minnesota

February, 2082

"When I grow up I'm going to be a veterinarian. Our teacher, Mrs. Jankowski, showed us this holodocumentary about elephants and how they're only alive in zoos now, but only Asian elephants. African elephants are extinct. There used to be hundreds of thousands of them in Africa, and at one time, probably even millions, but now they're all gone. It's so sad and we cried when it got to the part of these poachers shooting them. I could never imagine killing an elephant or any animal for that matter – but I could totally kill a poacher. I'm not kidding.

When I was little, my dad took me to this restaurant that had all these dead animal heads mounted on the walls, like deer, elk, and a moose – and there were all these chandeliers made out of antlers too. In the corner there was a giant, stuffed grizzly bear standing on his hind legs posed like it was attacking. It was huge. It must've been ten feet tall. I just stared at it and wondered what it must've been like when it was alive. I felt so bad for it, and in case you didn't know, they're extinct too – grizzlies. Grizzlies and polar bears – gone!

We were sitting at our table and this really old guy, the owner, comes up, and I asked him who killed all the animals. He said that he'd shot a few, and that his friends and family had shot some of the others. I asked him about the grizzly and he told me that his great-grandfather shot it over a hundred years ago. I got in big trouble when I said I wished the grizzly had killed him instead, but I didn't care. I'd never eat in a place like that. My dad should have known, but he was so clueless. He should have known better than to take me there.

He died a couple weeks ago in our garage when a big shelving unit fell on him. He was a meat eater. He had it coming."

Jeanette DeLuca, 41
Retired Teacher
Born: 2051
Died: 2089
Marion, Ohio

March, 2082

"It was fairly typical for kids in my elementary classrooms to range in age by a year, give or take. I started out teaching third graders, then I moved up to the fifth grade, and that's where I stayed until the elementary schools closed. I mean there were a few instances where a parent refused to hold back their child in the first grade, and those students may have been a tad less mature, but by the time they got to me, it was mostly fine, but my opinion is that maturity in the classroom has little to do with age – like so much else, I chalk it up to parenting. Then the post-Pollens arrived in my classroom, and everything - and I mean everything - changed. Throw out all the theories of learning, the pedagogical approaches, auditory, visual, kinesthetic – throw it all out, because this was a whole new paradigm – literally.

These kids are different."

Rebecca Tindall, 27
Single Mother

March, 2082

"I'm not gonna say Darcy is disrespectful. That's not really the right word, but she is direct. She doesn't suffer fools. She's smart, like off-the-charts smart, and she's not afraid to tell you when you're wrong about something. I remember back when she was about four years old, we went on a little hike at the nature center, and I pointed out this bird that was perched on a branch. I told her that I thought it was a gold finch, and she corrected me – that it was actually a western meadowlark – our state bird. She was really upset that I didn't know the difference between a finch and a lark. I asked her how many other birds she knew, and for the rest of the hike she correctly identified every bird, animal, and insect we came across. She was four! She even knew all the other state birds! I never taught her any of that stuff. After that I bought her the *Audubon Field Guide to North American Birds*, and when I gave it to her that was one of the few times she hugged me. To this day she's literally never without it. Oh, and thanks to Darcy I'm a vegetarian now because she will not tolerate meat in the house – not even fish.

A few months ago we hosted a hologram night, and my sister Brianna, Darcy's aunt, came over with pizza, but it was a meat lover's, you know, with pepperoni and sausage and what not. Darcy could smell it before the box was even open and she started screaming like a banshee and got so upset that she ran to the bathroom and threw up. Brianna was like, 'I knew your daughter was troubled, but I didn't know she was psycho!' and this, by the way, is typical of Brianna; it's like she enjoys provoking and stirring things up. I should never have invited her. So anyway, Darcy comes out of the bathroom and just glares at her. Brianna told her to wipe that hate off her face and that if she were her daughter she'd be properly disciplined. Then out of the blue Brianna's nose starts gushing blood. I grabbed a roll of paper towels and led her to the sink. I turned toward Darcy and mouthed the words; *stop this* and instantly Brianna's nose stops bleeding. This has happened two other times that I know of: once with a babysitter, and another time with an older boy in the neighborhood. I don't like talking about it, but this is something that Darcy can do to people when she's furious. Don't ask me how.

In spite of all this, she's a great kid, she really is: Quiet, smart, curious, so interesting to be around, and she loves animals – but she's... she can be cold. I love her so much. It's just...."

Gregory Felcynn, 48
Director of Statistical Analysis, U.S Census Bureau
Born: 2034
Died: 2089
Washington D.C.

April, 2082

"In 2070, the year after Pollen, the estimated population of the United States was 424 million. In 2080, the year of the last census, the population was 411 million. That's a population decline of 13 million people. If zero birth continues the curve will pitch toward the vertical as we reach exponential population decline. The dead are simply not being replaced! We're literally facing extinction, but you'd never know it if you paid any attention to what's going on in Washington.

During my closed-door hearing with Congress, I let the committee know that we need to ratchet up the urgency by multiple factors, but that was six months ago and I've yet to see any progress, and that's why I'm now going public. We're headed into uncharted territory, and we'll be faced with many unpleasant and unprecedented realities.

Not to sound alarmist, but… strike that… actually I'm ringing the bells – this is my clarion call: We're facing the inevitable collapse of civilization; our economy; our ability to effectively govern, defend, and police ourselves will become impossible; our energy infrastructure will fail; at some point, and ideally sooner rather than later, we'll have to dismantle our nuclear power plants and weapons, and store all radioactive materials in a safe and secure manner, and this alone is going to cost billions and billions of dollars. We've already had one melt-down with one of our nuclear-powered submarines on the Alaskan coast. There will be more if we don't act now.

The decimation of our medical infrastructure is inevitable; agricultural and transportation systems will cease to exist. In other words, extreme societal and individual hardship is inevitable, and these eventualities will most certainly hasten population decline.

The ramifications are mind boggling so prepare for the apocalypse! In seventy-five years the post-Pollens will be in their late-80s, and provided they have the same life expectancy as we pre-Pollens have – which seems unlikely given the extreme hardship the future holds – I estimate that humankind will be extinct in about eighty years – and I'm probably being overly optimistic."

Reverend Mark D. Hopper, 51
Evangelical Leader

May, 2082

"This was clearly the will of God, and we as a nation must repent. The elders and I have spent many hours, many days, and many nights locked away in prayer and contemplation. We've read the scriptures and prophecies – especially the Book of Revelation, and we've concluded that Pollen was indeed the second coming of Jesus Christ. We've also reflected upon our lives as soldiers for Christ and realize that we've fallen far short in being worthy of His glory, and that's why we've been left behind. We've repented our many sins of the heart, and our many sins of the flesh, and have accepted the Lord Jesus back into our hearts, and with His precious blood, we've been born-again. It is with great verve that we've recommitted ourselves to the fight for the souls of this nation and we will not rest until every man, every woman, and every child commits to His greater glory. Now, it has been revealed to me that when that day comes we shall again hear the cry of the newborn, and we shall rejoice when the babe suckles of his mother's milk, and that babe too shall be brought up to love the Lord Jesus Christ with all his heart and soul!

We are the shining city on that hill! We are the New Jerusalem! Our spiritual missionaries have been busy in the halls of Congress and in the halls of every capitol of every state in our great republic, spreading the word of God to our leaders, many of whom have gotten down on their knees and prostrated themselves before our Savior, and they too have repented their sins and have joined us in our crusade against the devil and his lies, against sin, against anarchy, and against atheism, all which come from the pits of hell!

We shall not be moved from our campaign, for our nation's salvation depends upon our victory, and when it becomes necessary, we will take up arms against those who would thwart us in our mission to heal our nation and the world through His precious blood."

Dr. Deborah Bernstein, 56
Research Scientist

May, 2082

"It's been thirteen years and post-Pollens have yet to show any signs of puberty. On the other hand, we pre-Pollens have now completely lost our ability to reproduce and the institute has concluded that this condition is permanent and irreversible. Ovaries have been absorbed by the body to the point of not existing, and it's the same with testes – they're simply gone. Our research has so far not provided any answers on how and why this has happened. As a species it would seem that our days are numbered. As concerns post-Pollens – we'll have to wait and see what happens. I'm optimistic about them because their reproductive organs continue to develop, but again, we can only speculate what's going to happen with these kids; we're in a holding pattern.

These days, in addition to leading the Global Fertility and Reproduction Restoration Institute, I'm also its lead booster and fund-raiser. Our federal funding was terminated in the last budget that was passed, so we now rely exclusively on gifts, donations, and endowments. Fund raising is an activity that I'm not all that well suited for – I'd much rather be looking through the eye-piece of a microscope – but as they say... you gotta do what you gotta do."

Julia Petyrkowski, (Post-Pollen Juvenile), 12
Born: 2070
Middle School Student
Augusta, Maine

May, 2082

"It was a long time ago, but I remember it like it was yesterday. About half-way through third grade this new kid arrived. He was really big, like easily the biggest kid in the school, and when I first saw him I thought that he was somebody's big brother who was dropping something off for a younger sib, like his little brother forgot his lunch or something. But it turned out that he was a new fifth grader and within a week everybody was scared of him because he was a total bully. His name was Tony, and I don't know what his problem was, but he liked picking on younger kids because I dunno, that's what bullies do, right? – Like he had something to prove.

So this one day we had a sub and she asked my best friend Sophie to take the attendance down to the office. Sophie asked if I could go with her but the sub said no even though that was totally allowed. Whatever. So Sophie leaves and she doesn't come back and the sub is thinking like, *Great! I've got a kid who's out wandering the halls,* but that's totally not Sophie at all! So she calls the office to let them know that Sophie's missing and to please send her back to class, but then she's all quiet while listening, then hangs up. Sophie doesn't come back so I asked her what happened and she said that Sophie's parents were picking her up and for me not to worry about it. So I thought-talked to Sophie and asked her what happened and she told me that the new kid came up behind her and shoved her really hard and that she hit her head on the drinking fountain and that she was bleeding. She had to get stitches.

A couple days later I stayed after school for a project, and after when I was walking home I saw Tony up ahead standing by the short-cut trail that goes through the field. I always take the short-cut, so when I got up to him he blocks my way with a stick he's got and tells me that I can't pass unless I give him something. I ignored him and kept going but he cut me off and held his stick at my face. I was so mad. I told him that he hurt my friend and that she had to get stitches. 'Oh yeah, that stupid girl,' he said. 'She got me kicked out of school.' I told him that he got himself kicked out of school for being such a bully and that he better not try that stuff with me. He asked, 'What are you gonna do?' and I said, 'Why don't you follow me and find out.' So I turned to walk and he followed. I wasn't even scared. I stopped just before the tree trunk bridge that crosses over the creek and he pushed me and said, 'You're goin' for a swim, little girl!' I faced him and maybe it was the look on my face but he backed away and I saw his fear. Then I knew. I stared at his chest and I don't know how or why, but I concentrated on his heart. I could hear and feel it beating and I imagined that I saw it, but it was so real and everything became like slow-motion. I don't know how but I knew that I had control of his heart. I felt his fear as it beat faster and faster. I focused so hard that I got dizzy, then I pointed at his chest and shouted, 'Stop!' He dropped like a puppet whose strings had been cut. I meant for him to stop: to leave me alone; to not be a bully and to stop hurting people.

I didn't mean to make his heart stop. I ran home crying and told my mom that I found a dead boy in the field. She believed me. So did everyone.

We call it Tony's Field now."

John Radner, 30
Activist/Conspiracy Theorist

June, 2082

"We thought it would be easier to achieve our goals from the inside rather than the outside, so we joined the Indiana National Guard, but in groups of five so as not to draw too much attention to ourselves. I was older than the average basic training recruit, so they picked me as platoon leader, and I saw to it that my four cohorts were appointed squad leaders. We cycled through basic and our platoon took every single training award, but more importantly, we'd won over our drill sergeants and everyone in our platoon to our cause. This was all the validation I needed and after that I knew that we were on the right track, and that we were on to something.

After basic training, we shipped out to Fort Leonard Wood, Missouri, for advanced infantry training, and once again I was appointed platoon leader. I busted ass: first one in, last one out… the whole nine yards. When I won the Base Commander Trainee of the Quarter Award, that drew the attention of the brass and they tried to talk me into transferring to Regular Army, but that was not part of the plan. It would have been way too difficult to start an insurrection at a regular army base, so no… the Indiana National Guard was the way to go. That was the goal, and that's where I ended up.

In five years I made master sergeant, which is the state record for achieving that rank. Since then they've practically put me in charge of security at Camp Atterbury. They literally handed me the keys to this place.

Now…I'm going to tick off a list of things the government has done that they've never come clean about: Pearl Harbor, the Kennedy Assassination, 9-11, the Trump Papers, the Second Secession, and the

Silicon Valley Massacres. All of these things have been thoroughly investigated and explained with an official government finding – otherwise known as a cover-up – and then there's the truth behind these incidences that ironically, always get spun into and dismissed as conspiracy theory.

All those government orchestrated events pale in comparison to Pollen – which is the motherlode of all deep state plots for population control – but they fucked-up, didn't they?! They fucked-up bad! The plan was to make only certain segments of the population sterile; not to make everyone sterile, but that's sure as shit what happened, right?! And there are some seriously pissed-off Americans out there that are demanding answers, and I'm one of them. But look at what's happening: evangelicals and their rapture bullshit; the scientific community and their neutron star theories! The government's reaction has been nothing more than paralyzation and malaise. But the most disturbing things to have come out of this catastrophe are the post-Pollens; there's something not right about them – you know it, and I know it.

It's now T-minus year 4 and counting until we make our move. Every month our ranks grow stronger as more and more highly motivated, highly dedicated personnel cycle in here at Camp Atterbury. Our goals are simple: find the truth, get the cure out into the open, and eradicate the post-Pollen population. We're four hundred strong and growing, and in the immortal words of the late, great President George W. Bush: 'You're either with us or against us.' Either way… we've got plans for everyone."

Dr. Ellitha Mais-Jackson, 63
Born: 2019
Died: 2089
Director, Detroit Institute of Arts
Detroit, Michigan

July, 2082

"An interesting phenomenon has transpired over the last couple of years in that people come into the museum and beeline to the works that depict babies, especially the Madonna and Child paintings in our collection – so much so that we've had to move these into the largest special exhibition galleries and manage the flow of people. It's completely understandable and heartbreaking really, to watch; young couples standing in front of Carolus-Duran's *The Merrymakers*, for example, or Giovanni Battista-Tiepolo's *Madonna and Child*, and how the Christ child stares out of the painting and looks directly into the crying eyes of these couples. People really respond to that one. Another strange thing as of late is that too many of our guests literally reach out and touch some of the paintings that depict babies and children, and we've had to up our security footprint to prevent this from continuing. This would happen occasionally in the old days, and we do have signage, but now it's become like an epidemic – hands off the art, people!

We were going to put together a special exhibition relating to infants, families, and parenthood but then found that it was impossible to get other museums and collectors to loan their works in this genre because demand is so great; everyone's asking but nobody's giving."

CHAPTER THREE – 2087 A.D.

<u>Dr. Deborah Bernstein, 60</u>
<u>Research Scientist</u>

<u>February, 2087</u>

"The reasons for dissolving the institute are many and complicated, but I'll give you the Cliff Notes: It was expensive and money was not coming in, and once it became obvious that we would never be able to restore fertility in the pre-Pollen population, we refocused and doubled our efforts toward studying post-Pollen physiology, but conspiracy theory and ignorance metastasized into some seriously ugly movements, and it became too risky to continue in our work. I traveled all over the country defending the institute and its mission at various engagements, but it eventually became too dangerous for me to appear in public. I actually had to hire bodyguards, but when the bomb went off in our University of Chicago labs and killed four of our scientists I decided that that was enough. I closed up shop.

I'm sad – sad and amazed at the speed at which everything is falling apart, and I'm aghast at how all these fringe groups have become mainstream, and how they've been able to hijack the conversation. Legitimate science has been relegated off to the side, indeed, we've become a pariah. Too many people believe that the scientific community is somehow responsible for Pollen, and that we were engaged in some nefarious plot to control the world's population. Actually it's difficult to keep up with the lunacy, so I don't bother anymore because each conspiracy is more stupid than the next, but on the other hand, I get it… I understand why it's happening, and the legitimate scientific community does bear some of the responsibility. Society needs answers to what happened, and we have not been able to provide any, so the dearth of information created a vacuum, and in swooped the conspiracies, the pseudo-science, and the religious and eschatological paranoia.

The bottom line is that after eighteen years and billions of dollars in research, we have no idea what happened. We're as mystified about Pollen today as the day we first started looking for answers. Sure, we know what it did to humankind, we just don't know how and why. I've been asked many times if I have any personal thoughts on what Pollen was all about, but my theories sound every bit as crazy as some of the wacky conspiracies out there – the difference though, is that mine have been informed by eighteen years of scientific research."

Andy Lerche, 17
Post-Pollen Juvenile
Born: 2070
Refugee
Sheridan, Wyoming

March, 2087

"We had to evacuate Sheridan because there were rumors of a large kill squad coming up the Tongue River. We can handle it when there's three or four of them, but a big group – no way. They just start shooting wildly, and when that happens, people die.

So we headed north toward Montana and crossed into a no trespass zone. It had been abandoned for a while so we thought it would be safe to rummage through a few of the houses to see if we could scavenge some supplies because we'd be trekking through some pretty rough country and the highway was not an option with all the check points. So we started rummaging and mostly there wasn't anything worth a shit, but then we went into the last house and bingo – we hit the jackpot: a pup tent, freeze-dried packets of food, animal-free protein product, tons of canned veggies, and a high-quality backpack; plus I found a great pair of boots that fit perfectly. We were ready to leave but there was an old barn nearby, and I told Donny and Wendy that we needed to at least check it out, and they agreed.

So we finally got the door jimmied open and it was crazy. There was an antique car from the 1920s with a combustion engine; it was an old Packard car, which I'd never heard of, that was absolutely huge but it only seated two people. People were so wasteful back in those days. I'd only seen cars like this in history books and I had no idea that they were so big; I mean, you can never tell from the holopics, and because it still had a combustion engine that made it highly illegal to own. We agreed that the owner must've had a special permit or something. There were tons of other things related to old cars in there, too; it was like walking into a museum.

Toward the back there was a small office, so we went in; kinda boring with just a desk and a couple of filing cabinets, but whatever… so I rummaged through the desk drawers and found an old .44 Magnum that was loaded. Wendy said that we should take it but Donny said no way and that we had other ways to defend ourselves which was true, so I put it back.

In one of the filing cabinets there was a huge stack of these old magazines that were filled with pictures of naked people doing things with each other. We decided that this was sex. We laughed at how stupid and ridiculous it looked; men with women, men with men, and women with women. Apparently people used to do sex with each other in lots of different ways, and with whoever. We wondered about it. Was it like when you were hungry and had to eat? We knew that people did it to reproduce, but we had no idea that there were so many different ways. Did people just stop what they were doing and make the sex with whoever they were with? Was it like, 'Oops! It's sex time! Get naked! Excuse me while I put my penis in here!' What made people want to do all these different things with the positions?! When animals do it, the male gets on top and humps and that's it… but the magazines showed all these different ways and body positions – it was hilarious and stupid, and we could not stop laughing… then it got boring.

We rummaged around the barn for a bit longer but we'd stayed way too long and we had to get a move on. It was almost dark by the time we left. We had to get to the safety of the forest and set up, but before we left, I went back to the office and opened the drawer with the gun. It was gone."

Matthew Delvin, 66
Writer

April, 2087

"L.A. has become a totally lawless shithole, and my house has been broken into way too many times. I couldn't take it anymore, so I hired a security firm to come out and guard my property, so the next day this giant, fuckin' skinhead goon shows up looking like a Nazi's wet dream. He's got his big, black E-350 Lectrochev parked diagonally across my driveway and I can't get by so I honk to get Klaus Dieter to move out the way. He looks down at me from the driver's seat, smirks, then flips me off, and I'm like, what the fuck!? I'm paying these people way too much money for attitude like that, so I vidicom the security firm and who answers but Klaus Dieter in his big, black Lectrochev.

'Oh hey, well whaddya know… it's you,' I said. 'Guess what? You're fired, asshole! Now get the fuck off my property.' Pretty much immediately he sees who he's talking to, so he disconnects, then jumps out of his Nazi-mobile and walks toward me. I climb out of my HydroLex, and I'm thinking, *what's this guy gonna do? Beat my ass?* And I'm just a little nervous, you know? He stops, but he's way too into my personal space like, our noses would be touching except his is seven inches higher than mine, and he says, 'You got some nice digs here, Mr. Delvin. I like the landscaping, I like the view. I really like the pool. I basically like everything about this place. In fact I like it so much that I'm gonna keep it and throw you the fuck out,' and I'm like, 'You can't do that! I'll call the police!' He scoffs, 'Police!? You seen any police around here lately? Lemme tell you something… in this neighborhood, I am the police. Go ahead and make your call. They ain't gonna do shit. In fact your precinct's been abandoned for quite a while now. But you knew that. That's why you called me.' I asked him if this was his M.O. now – you know, not guarding properties but stealing them, and he says, 'Only the ones I like – and I really, really like yours.' Then he unsnapped the guard on his holster and grabbed the stock of his pistol and says, 'But I'm not all that bad, Mr. Delvin. In fact, I'm actually gonna let you go inside and pack two suitcases, then I'll kindly escort you back to your vehicle under armed guard, because you know, this neighborhood has really gone to shit and I wouldn't want anything bad to happen to you.' Then he laughs at his clever irony… the fucker. What else could I do? He followed me inside, I packed my bags, then we walked back out to the driveway. Before I pulled away he says, 'And don't worry about a thing, Mr. Delvin. No one's ever gonna rob this place again. I'll see to that.'

So it's a good thing I've got a second home in Ventura, but I'm thinking that it's just a matter of time before somebody tries to steal this place too – so I bought a gun… and I learned how to shoot."

Edwin Mossbauer, 36
Motivational Speaker
Born: 2050
Died: 2089
Charleston, South Carolina

May, 2087

"I was 18 or 19 years old when it happened, and way too much into vaping Crystal-Lyth, Neo-Cannabis, HeavenSynth, and too many other drugs to mention throughout the entirety of my teenage years, so honestly the 60s are mostly a complete blank for me – the one exception of course being Pollen: It's been 18 years, and I still remember everything about that day, but I gotta tell you, after Pollen – drugs were boring. They didn't have the same effect, and trust me; I tried very hard to enjoy them again, so in a way, Pollen turned out to be a positive in that it got me off drugs for good, but the single, biggest bummer to come out of it, obviously is never having been able to father a child, so in a way, this crazy mix of experiences has put me where I am today.

I get the opportunity to speak to high school kids all over the country about addiction, but the most important aspect of what I do is not speaking, but listening. What's weird though is that this'll be my last year. Come June? No more high schools because the kids will have aged out. Isn't that weird!? I'll have to switch gears and move up to the college circuit now, or what's left of it, I guess.

A lot of people are freaked out about the post-Pollens but I think they're fascinating; they've got a lot to offer this world, and their voices are only just now starting to be heard. I'll tell you, it's pretty damn incredible to be living through these immense times of change, so when that coordinated mass school shooting happened in March, a part of me was not surprised – I mean, these things have been happening for so long that the media doesn't even pay attention to them anymore, but there's never been a mass shooting on this scale. Dozens of high schools, all over the country, raided in a coordinated and organized attack with military armaments. What the hell was that all about!? I was sad, outraged, and pissed-off, and I still am actually, I mean, it's all so senseless, and the fear that's been stoked by all these different groups – well here's your end result – good, innocent people getting slaughtered. But when news started filtering out about how many of these fanatical militia idiots were killed during the attack by the post-Pollen kids who were simply minding their own business, sitting in their classrooms and just, you know… being students… how'd they do that!? How were these kids able to turn the tables, defend themselves, and kill so many of these lunatic militiamen? And these kids weren't armed! They've got something we pre-Pollens don't have and that, I believe, is why so many people are afraid of them. It's a terrible thing, what fear can do to people."

Paige Vanderzahne, 64
Entrepreneur
Born: 2025
Died: 2089
Dallas (Bluffview), TX

June, 2087

"Things are fine and I honestly don't understand all this fuss about crime. I mean, there's always going to be crime at some level, right? People just need to get a grip – find a hobby, volunteer, have a cocktail with friends! Remember that old saying, 'Idle hands are the devil's playthings.' Our problems stem from the fact that people are bored and have become mentally and physically lazy, so they go out and look for trouble. It's all so ridiculous.

Sure, Pollen was a tragedy, and it's sad that people can't have babies anymore, but take a look at all these animals (I'm sorry, that's what they are) who're causing all this trouble. It's actually a blessing that we've been spared from their ability to reproduce; I mean can you imagine what their children would have been like!? Generation after generation of lazy and violent reprobates, but all that has come to a grinding halt now, hasn't it – good, I say!

I'm not too vain to admit that I'm 64 years old. I'm active, I'm fit, I play tennis and golf, and I even take the skiff out now and then when it's not too windy. All I'm saying is that people need to stay active, but if that's not your thing, then go to the library! Read a book, get a new perspective, learn something, and for god's sake... better yourself!"

Rebecca Tindall, 33
Single Mother

June, 2087

"I was in the school cafeteria zeroing out the Q-System when suddenly there was a huge explosion that shook the whole building. The lights flickered and drywall and dust came flying down, then everything went dark. My eyes adjusted and only dim light filtered down from the skylights. I heard these pop, pop, pops, smelled gunpowder, then I knew what was going on. I'd been through a couple school shootings when I was a kid, so I remembered my training and waited for the auto-shields to come down but they never did, then I started to panic. I was not going to leave that school without Darcy but she'd said something before about having extended lab and would not be coming to lunch. The labs were in the area from where I heard the gunshots, but it was hard to tell because it was dim, and smoke started filling the room, and the alarms were going off, and my ears were ringing, and I was really disoriented, but I had to get to Darcy, so I headed toward the doors, and Tiff and Gerry are yelling at me to get down, but I wasn't having it.

I ran down the hall toward the quad and I looked out the window and saw an army tank and soldiers and they were shooting at the school, but a lot of the soldiers were writhing on the ground with their heads all bloody. I got to the lab but it was empty – no Darcy – so I turned to leave, but there was a soldier standing in the doorway and he told me to lie down. He asked me if I was a teacher, and I told him that I worked in the cafeteria, and he said that was just as bad. I was laying on my stomach and I got queasy and I felt like I was gonna throw-up, and I don't know where I got the courage, but I asked him why he was doing this, and if he had any kids of his own, I mean, he looked like he could've been a father – just a normal looking guy in camouflage. Then

I heard struggling. I looked up and blood was pouring from his eyes, nose, and ears, and he was scared, I mean, I could see it in his eyes. He was trying to keep his pistol down, but it was like someone had taken control of his arm, and he was straining every muscle but the pistol went to his head and it's like I didn't even hear the shot – his brains just sprayed all over the wall and he crumpled to the ground in a heap. Then I threw up acid and bile.

Max, one of Darcy's best friends, ran into the lab and grabbed me by the arm and told me that we had to leave. I told him I wasn't going anywhere until I found Darcy, but he told me that she'd already gotten out and that he'd take me to where she was and that I had to trust him, so we bailed. I don't remember much about how we got to the hideout.

So there they were – a bunch of the post-Pollen students waiting in this big pole barn near the old train station. I was amazed actually at how many of them had gotten out alive. Max took me to Darcy, and she was sitting on the ground and staring straight ahead. None of the kids were talking and it was really quiet, so I sat next to her but I could see by the look on her face that she didn't want to talk, so I kept quiet too. It turned out that a few of Darcy's teachers and schoolmates were killed, but that way more soldiers had died.

We had to leave Kearney and we eventually made it up to Canada where things are actually normal and people aren't going around killing each other. I tried talking to Darcy about everything that had happened, but she won't talk about it. She only said that she misses the voices of her dead friends.

We didn't have time to pack much of our stuff. It gets cold here at night. I wish there was more to do in this camp. It's pretty spartan. We just sit around all day in these drafty, old huts and sometimes I play cards with the other adults. They have counselors and tutors for the kids but none of them are interested; they just sit there clustered in circles and mind-talk. They're peculiar but we're used to it. What's sad is that they were a couple months away from graduating but after the attack everything shut down, not just the school but the whole town, practically. Darcy's principal told us during a Q-call that she'd contact us when they'd reopen but there's no way we're going back.

Yesterday Darcy came up to me and said the strangest thing, she said, 'You're not going to be around much longer, mother,' and I told her that that wasn't true, and that I had a lot of life in me yet. 'No. You don't understand, but you will... you'll see,' she said, then walked away so matter of fact as if she'd just told me the time of day – typical Darcy... friendly one minute, cold as ice the next.

I wish I had someone to talk to."

Dr. Deborah Bernstein, 61
Research Scientist

July, 2087

"It's reasonable to assume that an ant crawling on the sidewalk wouldn't have any idea why it suddenly sparked out of existence in a burst of searing pain, but the cruel adolescent aiming a magnifying glass down onto that unfortunate ant certainly would. I've been reticent about sharing what I believe brought Pollen on because I don't have enough information to form even a hypothesis. After all these years I can only speculate, and I'm not in the business of speculation. Now I can tell you plenty about what it's done to us as a species – we pre-Pollens suffer through the absolute and irreversible destruction of our reproductive systems, and this inevitably leads to our extinction, while the post-Pollens have so many differences in physiology from us that they can be justifiably classified as a different species – an abrupt jump that leaves we pre-Pollens in the evolutionary dustbin of history.

I believe that Pollen was a bioengineering magnifying glass that sparked Homo sapiens out of existence, and that something unimaginable, with an intelligence we cannot even begin to fathom, came along and sentenced us to death with their proverbial magnifying glass. Can I prove this? Absolutely not, but as far as I know, nothing like this has ever happened to any other species in the entire history of life on this planet. This was a singular anomaly and I do not believe that it was an accident. Pollen was so precise, so targeted, and so successful that how could it have been anything other than the act of a super-intelligent, extraterrestrial life form? I can't think of anything else that could have caused this catastrophe, and just saying this puts me at great risk of professional ridicule because again, it's pure speculation. But at this point I've literally got nothing left to lose.

You've heard the old saying, the lunatics are running the asylum? Well, that's never been more true than today, so if you can't beat 'em, join 'em... and after all these years, maybe that's finally what I've done."

John Radner, 35
Activist/Conspiracy Theorist

September, 2087

"I'm still connected and I've been watching what they've been saying on the Fox/Sinclair/Max Holonet, and it sucks how they've turned on me with all their bullshit, so I guess it's understandable why I've become so hated, but the people need to understand and not buy into the lies and conspiracy. When I step back and actually think about what it is I've tried to accomplish… well, on its face, there's no actual way to put a positive spin on killing teenagers with military grade weapons. But these are not normal teenagers; they're post-Pollen scum and they need to be eradicated from the Earth. That's a fact, plain and simple, and to my mind there's no argument! Case closed!

The people need to know and understand what these freaks are capable of. I've seen things that have literally curdled my blood. I witnessed an entire squad of soldiers storm a high school's media center, only to watch their eyeballs explode out of their sockets. I've experienced the intensity of their vibrations, and it's because of them that my right arm dangles from my shoulder like a useless goddamn noodle. The pain has dulled over the last week, but it flares up so bad sometimes that it feel like my very molecules are being ripped to shreds, especially when I try to sleep.

I ordered my company to go on without me and to carry on in the search and destroy mission, and the numero uno thing we've learned is that we've got to be smart and stealthy – to travel light and to keep our footprint small, because these post-Pollens… they've got advantages. They know things so I'm keeping my thoughts to a minimum and operating more on impulse. I ordered Delta Company to do likewise and to split up into platoon-sized recons and to maintain radio silence.

I can feel these post-Pollen motherfuckers getting into my head with their whispers, taunts, and lies. They know where I'm hiding, but I'll wait 'em out. I've set up a perimeter, and I hope to god – OH, I HOPE TO GOD that they try and breach it – the Claymore mines and trip wires I've set up will take care of 'em and after they've been blown to smithereens my arm will heal and the pain will go away, but right now they've got a lock on me, I know that for a fact, and that's why my arm is still fucked-up, but it's just a matter of wills and I promise anyone who cares to listen – my will is stronger.

I've got three days of rations left, and I ran out of potable water yesterday, so I'll recon after sunset for more. I didn't have time to map out my booby traps but no matter; I've got that array locked down to memory, point-blank, cut and dry, sure as shit. There's a stream about a kilometer from my encampment and I'll bring my purification kit. I've got this. I've so got this. Oooo-rah, motherfuckers! Come get some!"

Gregory Felcynn, 53
U.S. Census Bureau

October, 2087

"As is the case with so many other governmental entities, the U.S. Census Bureau has ceased to exist, so I no longer have access to reliable data, but I've been in this game for a long time, so… given that an average of 7 million people in the U.S. die every year, and that we've had zero birthrate for the last 18 years, I estimate that if we were able to conduct a reliable census in 2090, we'd see another significant drop in the population – well under 400 million. It hasn't been below 400 million since 2050.

I'm not at all surprised at how quickly things have fallen apart, but the executive, the legislative, and the military have certainly kept chugging along, haven't they?! But these politicians have always been slick in the dark arts of self-preservation – anything goes when it comes to maintaining power. The judicial has ceased to exist, so checks and balances have gone out the window, and that by the way, is why it was so easy to declare martial law. In every major city, law and order is maintained by private security outfits, but that's a farce too because a lot of these are really nothing more than extortion rackets. A few National Guard units have mutinied and transformed into well-equipped militias that are wreaking havoc, mostly in the south and the Great Plains, and all of these seem to be led by deranged, quasi-military conspiracy theorists with some seriously disturbed agendas. A lot of people are dying out there for some genuinely stupid reasons, but you know, the well-heeled in their gated communities seem to be immune from all the troubles… I know… big surprise, right? But I believe that we've been headed in this direction for years, and Pollen, finally, is the cow that kicked the lantern over – our Franz Ferdinand moment that pushed us off into the crazy.

I'm constantly asked why I've stuck it out this long... why I haven't fled the country for safer places, like Canada or Sweden, because let's face it, it's not like things are going to improve after the next election. We don't even conduct elections anymore... we're stuck with the sorry leadership that we've got, but in spite of everything, I still love this country. I love the land and the place where I grew up. I was raised by two loving parents in a small town with small town values and that's where I plan on drawing my last breath.

It's not going to take much longer for this whole kit and caboodle to come crashing down, but no matter what happens... I'm not going anywhere. I'm going to stick it out right here in the good old U.S. of A... or at least what'll be left of it."

Reverend Mark D. Hopper, 67
Evangelical Leader

October, 2087

"A major battle in this holy war for the souls of this nation has been won in the White House today where I met with the First Family, and I have been given permission to share that after a meeting of minds, a period of fellowship, and some mutual counsel, I led the President of the United States of America in the prayer of salvation, and he has accepted the Lord Jesus into his heart. His sins have been washed away with the precious blood of Jesus, and he's been born again, ready to serve the Lord. I believe that it'll be through the leadership of this blessed man of God that our nation will become whole again. The President has set the example, and America will surely look upon his leadership as a fulfillment of prophecy, and the people of this country will also repent and seek the loving embrace of redemption.

Our missionaries continue to minister in the state capitals across this great land, and although we are, at this time, a nation divided, it has been revealed to me that millions upon millions will turn away from the influence of the devil and his angels and seek out the Lord! All this I claim in the blessed name of Jesus! Amen!"

The Honorable Kendall McClellan, 70
Born: 2017
Died: 2089
United States Senator, Kentucky (R)
Washington D.C.

November, 2087

"There are a lot of exaggerations, fabrications, and outright lies being perpetrated by the elite members of media, but this has been going on for decades. These sowers of discord have one goal in mind, and that's to confuse the good and god-fearing citizens of this country – all who know that Congress has their back, that the President has their back, and that we're united in our commitment in fighting terrorism, lawlessness and crime, and maintaining unity and order.

In fact, never in the 311-year history of our great nation has there been a more united effort in serving the needs of the people, and I could list a hundred outstanding bills that the President has signed into law that benefit the citizens directly, first and foremost of which was the abolition of the IRS and making it illegal for the US Government to collect taxes from the good and hardworking people of this country. This tax relief will go a long way toward allowing the people to defend themselves against the tyranny that's being perpetrated by the atheists, the leftists, and extremist cartels that have been roaming the homeland in an attempt to tear the very fabric of our nation apart.

Security has improved measurably: the weapons are stronger, the walls are higher, and the technology is smarter, and I'm proud to announce that all these counter-measures will surely allow us to prevail over our enemies. God bless the people, the President, and the United States of America."

CHAPTER FOUR – 2089 A.D.

Johnathan Jerome Quinn
June 30, 2089

"Here is the only place in this collection of stories where I felt it appropriate to include my own personal accounting, for the calamity that I myself witnessed was too strange and incredible to leave off these pages, for it was on June 22, 2089 when every single pre-Pollen human across the entirety of the Earth simply ceased to be.

I was a few miles north of Ventura, California, riding my Lectrocycle along Coastal Highway 1. I pulled off onto a scenic overlook for a break. It was an hour before nightfall and I noticed a few other travelers who shared my intention of getting some rest. I grabbed my rucksack and walked a few paces onto the beach, unrolled my sleeping bag, ate the contents of a decomp-MRI, then settled in.

There were twenty-five or so other people within a two-hundred yard radius, a few traveling alone like myself, and others assembled in twos and threes. These were all homeless refugees: people who had lost their properties to militias, fraudulent security firms, and countless other predatory acts. The feeling on the beach was that of an uneasy détente – a *'you leave me alone, and I'll leave you alone'* feeling. Some went about their business in complete obliviousness, while others eyed their surroundings with deep suspicion. The guy closest to me pulled a gun halfway out of his bag and warned me to keep my distance. I told him that he had nothing to worry about – from me, anyway. I turned my attention toward the sea and watched the red orb of the sun slowly descend, then deform as it melted into the horizon, and wink-out in a flash of green a second before it dipped below the vast Pacific. I then laid down with my hands clasped behind my head and watched the sky settle down into a deep and dark violet blue with its billions of stars arching their way across infinity. I nodded off.

It was the strong scent that jarred me awake, followed quickly by the collective moan and elation of my fellow travelers. The sky flashed and shimmered in a wild and iridescent array of colors and tones, while strange, terrible, and colorful clouds billowed and roiled in a furious tempest above, but there was no wind – not even the slightest breeze. The ocean was still and reflected the chaos above. Pollen had returned, but because I had not been exposed the first time, I was apparently immune from the calamity that transpired over the next few minutes. I turned my gaze from the sky and onto my fellow travelers. Their elation was immediate, and they greeted the return of Pollen with an enthusiasm that catapulted them to their feet, their arms desperately reaching toward the roiling and boiling chaos of colors above. They inhaled the perfume with deep and panicked breaths, and many openly wept with joy – then, as quickly as they'd jumped to their feet, they were quieted and stilled, frozen in place, their faces surpassing the pleasure and pain of ecstasy.

I felt nothing and was free to walk about and observe. I went toward my closest neighbor, the fellow with the gun, who looked to be in his mid to late 60s; hearty, shortish in stature, with a slight belly, and a face etched by wind and sea. The tears that stained his cheeks were the first indication that something strange had happened; instead of leaving wet trails, they left deep furrows, like a stream of water through wet sand. I spoke and asked him if he was okay, but he didn't answer. Instead his arms crumbled and collapsed off his shoulders, followed by his head, torso, and thighs – only his calves remained upright. He'd been turned to dust – his blue shorts and American flag tee-shirt lay crumpled, partially buried under his sandy remains. I scanned the beach and saw that I was now alone, surrounded only by the blankets, bags, and small encampments evenly strewn and scattered like so much flotsam and jetsam. A gust of wind interrupted the calm and puffs of dust rose up from each pile.

I watched and bore witness to the end – the annihilation of humanity was orchestrated with a tenderness akin to a kiss – it was horrible.

I do not have the words to convey the terror I felt standing suddenly alone on that beach with the strong scent still permeating the air, and the terrible, multi-colored clouds roiling above. I only knew that Pollen had returned, only this manifestation destroyed every human being on Earth – or so I thought at the time.

I had heard so much about the Pollen of 2069. The friends I'd made over the years all had a *where I was and how it affected me* story, and all of them without exception, were happy and eager to share what they'd experienced, but one story sounded much like the other: they'd woken up, went outside, stared upward at the heavenly marvels, and experienced the intoxicating euphoria of the scent that stopped them dead in their tracks. Later they'd come to learn that they'd been rendered sterile, and although this made many of them profoundly sad, a gradual resignation settled in. I thought of their reactions as being similar to the death of a loved one – the pain is intense at first, then it eventually gives way to a mild and sorrowful nostalgia. This Pollen gave them a lightning-quick fix of that same euphoria, then killed and disposed of them seconds later in a most inexplicable way: they simply ceased to be.

It was a couple days later I learned that, like me, the post-Pollens had survived this second Pollen, and that all of their troubles with the most radical of the pre-Pollens—the fears, conspiracy theories, and mass murders—had also turned to dust and simply ceased to be.

I got down on my knees and reached for my neighbor's clothes lying there in his dust. I pulled the wallet from his shorts and found his ID. His name had been Matthew Delvin and he was a member of a writer's guild. He owned a house in Ventura. I decided on the spot to ride to that house and see what I could learn about this unfortunate soul who, just a few hours prior, had threatened me with a pistol."

<u>Dawn Leonard, 19</u>
<u>Post-Pollen Female</u>
<u>Reed, Oklahoma</u>

<u>June, 2089</u>

"There's nobody around anymore. I haven't seen anybody in days. I've been going around and opening barns and pens and letting all the livestock out. They'll starve otherwise, and what I've been doing might not be right, but the dreams... they're telling me otherwise.

I don't understand what's happened. Where is everybody?"

Andy Lerche, 19
Post-Pollen Male
Montana

June, 2089

"Of course we defended ourselves! We weren't gonna just roll over, but they were relentless. And we never did anything to deserve their hate, but none of that seemed to matter – you can't reason with crazy. We just wanted to be left alone, to live in peace, and to get on with our lives. I personally had never hurt anyone prior to the militias and kill squads. What bothered me most though was the stupidity and how they just made shit up about us, and worse was how many people actually believed all their bullshit. Anyway, by then it seemed like we'd been on the run forever with these lunatics always in hot pursuit.

So Donny and Wendy and I were in Montana near the Idaho border. By this time we had teamed up with another small group of post-Pollens: Margaret, Del, Mike, and their guide Tom, who was a few years older than us. Margaret and Del assured us that Tom was cool, but while they were talking, Del thought-talked me and said he wasn't a hundred percent on the guy and that there was something about him he didn't trust. I told Wendy and Donny to be on the lookout for anything funny, and they agreed. Tom told us about a lodge that had been abandoned a while ago and said that it was really remote, like too far out of the way for anyone to bother us if we went there, so we agreed that it was worth checking out. We found it after a few days' hike. We broke in and lucky for us, it had a pantry that was filled to the brim with canned and dry goods that could've easily lasted through the summer. What we didn't know was that the whole thing was a set-up.

So we're all sitting in the great room trying to work things out – guard duty, sleeping schedules, cooking, cleaning, all that stuff – and there's this big fireplace in the middle of the room and Tom suggests that we start a fire because, as he said, it was kinda dark and gloomy, but we nixed that idea outright because obviously smoke coming out of the chimney would've been a dead giveaway, right? I mean, that's just common sense – you don't just start a fire in the fireplace of a building you just broke into – and that he even suggested it put me on edge – plus the place had electricity and we'd turned a few of the lights on, so I don't know what he was talking about. After the meeting we ate and then decided to get some rest, but we agreed that a couple of us would have to pull guard duty. Tom's arm shot up to volunteer and that's when I pretty much had him pegged, I mean my radar was seriously pinging on him! I thought-talked Donny and Wendy and they agreed to stay awake just in case. Tom and I walked outside and by then it was night, but there was a full moon that was so bright you could've read a book under it. He suggested that I walk a beat around the back of the lodge and he'd walk the front. I didn't really see a problem with that, so I agreed.

It was chilly for a summer night but really beautiful with all the hills and mountains around, and I was actually feeling pretty good because my belly was full for the first time in a long time, and even though I was a little nervous about Tom, I kinda just let it go, thinking that maybe I'd been a little paranoid. I guess I was just enjoying my solitude.

About an hour goes by and I heard a pop and saw a flare shoot up over the front side of the lodge. *Tom!* I thought… *that fucker!* I ran around to the front and as soon as I turned the corner I heard the crack of gunshots. There was a kill squad in the field out past the parking lot and their bullets whizzed and slammed into the building just over my head. I turned and hauled ass to a door that I had propped open earlier just in case. Wendy and Donny came blazing out with our gear ready to go, when this… thing happened… it was so bizarre. The sky just lit up, and at first we thought it was the aurora borealis, but this quickly became something much different. We're all looking at the sky and it was like weather from another planet, like fucking Jupiter or some shit! All these clouds like I'd never seen before, in all these different colors, and the most powerful storm I'd ever seen looked like it was about to hit, but everything was so quiet and still. Then this strong perfume smell came out of nowhere. We just looked at each other like, *what the fuck!* – and then … nothing... I have absolutely no memory of anything that happened after that. We'd all passed out right there behind the lodge; the three of us.

When Donny and I came to, Wendy was already awake. She said, 'You're not gonna believe this, but they're gone.' 'Who's gone?' Donny asked, and she said, 'The kill squad, dummy! I mean aren't you wondering, just a little, why we're still alive? I am!' She pulls out her .44 Mag and we followed her around to the front. She showed us Tom's clothes, which were laying there crumpled in the middle of the parking lot in a pile of dust along with his flare gun. Then she took us out to the field from where the kill squad had been firing at me and it was the same thing: piles of camouflage gear, uniforms, backpacks, night-vision goggles, boots, weapons, you name it – and every pile covered in dust. None of this made any sense. Donny thought it was a trap, but that didn't make sense either because they would have found us lying unconscious behind the lodge and simply killed us. Wendy said that what happened was probably another Pollen, like the one our parents went through before we were born. I didn't even think of that; I mean that never even occurred to me – I was just too fucked-up and confused. Then Margaret, Del, and Mike walk out of the lodge toward us looking every bit as confused as us. Donny pointed over at Tom's pile of clothes and said, 'You guys could sure use some lessons in how to pick friends!'

We had no idea how long we'd been out, a few hours maybe? And none of us really had any idea what the hell had happened, although what Wendy said about it being another Pollen kind of made sense in a sick and twisted way. I can tell you one thing for sure though: that was the weirdest, most fucked-up, topsy-turvy day of my entire life.

And don't even get me started on how we'd all had basically the same, bizarre dreams while we were passed out."

Phillip Meijerson, 19
Post-Pollen Male
Minnesota

July, 2089

"I had just finished letting a few antelope out of the drone transport. It was on land that was adjacent to the nuclear power plant and there were literally thousands of acres for them to graze. The Mississippi was nearby, too – a good, clean water source for them, so the release location was ideal. For the last couple of weeks a few of us had been releasing animals from the zoo – at least the ones that we knew would survive in our climate. The animals indigenous to Africa and the tropics – we hadn't figured that out yet, so we'd be caring for them until we came up with a plan. All we knew was that in the meantime they'd need caring for, and we were not going to allow them to just simply die, and this by the way, is one of the reasons I've always hated zoos: when something terrible happens it's always the animals that suffer worst.

So it was a warm, sunny day but I looked and a few miles off in the direction of the power plant I saw a circle of thick fog off in the distance that was rotating pretty quickly, and the crazy thing is that this vortex hadn't been there five minutes prior. I walked toward it because I'd never seen anything like it! It looked like a slowly rotating tornado but really big, like maybe F3 in size, but the top was so incredibly high that it actually looked like it was coming from outside the atmosphere, I mean this thing was miles high and I kept walking toward it because how often does one encounter a… I don't know what to call it… a space tornado? It was fascinating, but the closer I got, the colder it got, then I noticed a peculiar odor, and it hit me: it suddenly felt like my head was being squeezed in a vice, and I had the most intense migraine I'd ever experienced. I'd never been in such incredible pain – so bad that I doubled over and began to vomit, then I turned around and ran away, and as soon as I got away from the odor the migraine stopped.

I feel like I was being warned to stay away from the vortex. I should have known because looking back on it, it did actually resemble the clouds during second Pollen, with lots of different colors and all; that and the fact that I'd been having these weird dreams that kind of connected to these things.

Over the next few days I released more animals near that same location, and the vortex was always still there, rotating over the power plant, and you can bet that I kept a respectful distance. Then one day it was gone – and so was the power plant. Not a trace; it simply wasn't there anymore."

<u>Julia Petyrkowski, 19</u>
<u>Post-Pollen Female</u>
<u>Augusta, Maine</u>

<u>August, 2089</u>

"Sophie and Trudy and I have been going around and releasing dogs and cats that had been trapped inside houses. At first we were feeding and watering them and then letting them go, but then Trudy came up with the idea of dumping piles of their kibble on the front porches and driveways so now we do that along with turning the spigots on to a trickle and putting their water bowls under the stream. Sometimes it's really heartbreaking because the dogs want to follow us, and let's face it, the little ones; the chihuahuas, the pugs, the toy poodles, they basically have a zero percent chance of surviving more than a couple of weeks, although I did see that a chihuahua had joined a small pack of dogs near Vine Street, and it looked like she was holding her own just fine, but it's mostly the bigger dogs that have formed packs. And yes, we've already seen more than our share of half-eaten dogs and cats with buzzards crowding around their carcasses. Coyotes have been skulking around too and feasting away. I guess what we're witnessing is nature doing its thing, but we figure that it's much better to allow these dogs and cats out to fend for themselves, rather than allow them to starve trapped inside their homes. Things are mostly okay now but I worry when food starts getting scarce. I'm afraid it's going to be a free-for-all, but we're doing our best to keep them all fed and this effort takes up a big part of our day. We won't be able to keep this up forever, though. We've also been going into the abandoned grocery stores and dumping piles of kibble behind the stores because we've learned that dogs will basically shit where they eat, and it's better to have them shitting behind the building rather than in front.

Frankly I'm amazed at how quickly nature is taking over. Tall weeds are growing through all the cracks of the sidewalks and streets, and deer, moose, and other wildlife that you'd never expect to see in the city, or perhaps never noticed prior to second Pollen... they're now out and about doing their thing.

It's so quiet around here now. I miss my family, especially my mother. We were close, and it's still difficult when I think about what I saw when I woke up after second Pollen: my mom and dad's clothing and dust lying next to each other on the deck. I could tell that they'd been holding hands. But we're forming new families; I mean we have to if we're going to survive. I guess we're a lot like the dogs in how we're forming packs. Augusta used to have about twenty-thousand people, but now there are maybe, I don't know... a thousand – and it's only us now, the post-Pollens. Everyone's the same age. It's strange. There's no chaos or anything, not like before, but I'm proud to say that Augusta was mostly spared from a lot of the craziness that other parts of the country experienced.

I love that there's been an overall concern for the animals since second Pollen. We've noticed other people helping them out too and there are a lot of people at the petting zoo and the aquarium caring for the animals and sea life, so that's a good thing. There are people over at the water treatment plant as well, so I can only assume that that's in good hands – I hope so, anyway.

We moved into Blaine House, the governor's mansion. I know stupid, right? But there's actually a good reason: we started growing a big garden with lots of herbs and vegetables, and the property is surrounded by a tall fence which helps to keep out the deer, the rabbits, and other animals that would feast on what we're growing.

In order to feed ourselves we have to become farmers. We've been reading a lot of books on farming, food preservation, and canning. A lot of the grocery stores are getting pretty empty, and we've got to figure this out or we're going to starve, but I think we can do this. I'm optimistic."

Darcy Tindall, 19
Post-Pollen Female
Excerpts from an Interview
Broadcast over Multiple Platforms
Medicine Hat, Alberta

Q: When did you start having the dreams?

Darcy: For as long as I can remember, but they got really intense starting about four years before second Pollen. At first they didn't make any sense because I didn't have the context, and they were so far outside my day-to-day experience. It was like being in a foreign country and not knowing the language – I had to quickly learn and keep up with what it was I was seeing because these dreams... although bewildering, they were also lucid and visual. Some were actually more like nightmares and once they started to make sense, it was hard to process what I thought was going to happen.

Q: What you thought was going to happen?

Darcy: They don't provide answers. They're not like movies. They're more like images, and often really disturbing.

Q: Did they give you a clue that there would be a second Pollen?

Darcy: Yes, and clue is a good word because again the dreams don't come right out and provide answers.

Q: So what did you see in these dreams about second Pollen?

Darcy: I saw the clouds with dust blowing across a vast expanse.

Q: What else can you tell us about the dreams?

Darcy: I don't find it very interesting talking about the dreams per say. What is interesting though is that they've set me on a path of research and I've learned a great many things, and in so doing I've unearthed a lot of knowledge that's been lost to the ages. In case you haven't noticed these last few years have not exactly been a time of enlightenment.

Q: To say the least. What's the biggest thing that you can share about the dreams in conjunction with the research you've conducted? Is there like one big take away?

Darcy: During my research I learned that earlier this century an object was discovered flying at an incredibly high rate of speed near Jupiter's orbit. Astronomers back then determined that it was going way too fast for the gravity of our sun to have propelled it to that rate of speed, and armed with that, combined with its trajectory, they were able to correctly determine that this celestial body had come from outside of our solar system, and this was a historic first in astronomical circles. They named it Oumuamua which means scout in Hawaiian, and that name, as it turned out, was actually quite perfect. But they got pretty much everything else about it wrong; it was written-off as merely an asteroid... but that's not was it was.

Dawn Leonard, 19
Reed, Oklahoma

August, 2089

"I was pretty isolated because our grid had been destroyed by the militia a couple years ago, and the council was always too afraid to have it repaired, so I had no way of communicating, but I'd gotten used to it. At the same time, I was fed up with not knowing what the hell had happened to everybody, and even though I knew I was out of range, I tried calling out with thought-talk but no one responded – big surprise there, so I finally decided to drive out to Magnum to see if I could find anybody. When I got there all I saw was little piles of clothes strewn all over the place. The sheriff's Lectrochev was parked at Telly's restaurant with the driver's door open. *That's careless*, I thought, so I went over to it and his uniform, boots, utility belt, and pistol were just lying there a few feet away. *What did they all do?* I thought, *take off their clothes and run wild into the night?* I mean I seriously had no idea what had happened!

I went over to the high school and broke in. I needed to find some of the addresses of my post-Pollen school mates. I had quit school back in the 10th grade because of all the bullying and harassment of some of the upper classmen, and I had lost touch with a lot of my post-Pollen friends, but there were only a few of them in Magnum anyway, maybe a hundred, and I knew that quite a few had been killed. So I found what I was looking for and set out, but then I turned down East Van Buren and I saw Jesse Wayne walking toward North Michigan surrounded by about a hundred dogs. I honked and I thought he was gonna shit when he saw me. 'What happened? Where is everybody?' I asked, and he said, 'Whaddya mean? How could you not know? You been living under a rock?' 'Kind of,' I said. "I've been living in an old bomb shelter.' He just looked at me and said, 'You really don't know, do you?' and I yelled at him, 'NO! I'M TELLING YOU! I DON'T!' I shouldn't have yelled because a bunch of the dogs began to bark and he had to calm them down. 'Hop out and give me a hand with these guys,' he said. 'And don't worry, they're friendly. We've got nothing but time and it's a long story.'

So he told me everything and I couldn't believe what I was hearing.

As it turned out there were twenty-eight post-Pollens still alive in Magnum and they'd been busy letting all the pets out of people's homes, and some had gone to the outlying farms like I'd been doing and releasing livestock. Later, Jesse and I met up with everybody in front of the old post office and it was really nice seeing so many of my old friends again. Brandy Joe was sure that I'd been killed, and he gave me one of his famous, toothy, crooked smiles, and a big hug and that felt so good that I began to cry, and then everybody piled on. I'd never been one for big displays of affection, but it was like all the stress that I'd been going through over the last few years had been lifted right there and then, and I finally felt safe for the first time in I don't know how long. I just sat on the bench and wept. Karen put her arm around me and told me that everything would be okay, and I told her I know, and that's why I'm crying. 'These are tears of joy, girl!' and everybody laughed. But I was sad too; sad for all the people who were no longer with us… and I was sad for some of the pre-Pollens who'd been good and supportive. They'd risked so much and now they were gone.

So I guess it's all over now – the discrimination, the bullies, the radicals, the militias… and there's other things I'm not gonna miss – like being accused of witchcraft for one. And I'm not gonna miss those 'Christians' at that church outside of Reed who'd follow me around and harass me 24/7. Looking back on everything, I guess I'm lucky to be alive – but I had a few tricks up my sleeve that I wasn't afraid to use – and I had more than one hiding place.

The next day I got my stuff out of the bomb shelter. Brandy Joe helped. A bunch of us are bunking up at the Quartz Mountain Resort a few miles outside of town. There's a lot of food for now… but we've got some things to think about."

<u>Andy Lerche, 19</u>
<u>Montana</u>

<u>October, 2089</u>

"The power went out at the lodge, so Del and Donny and I tried to get this old, giant gas generator started. No luck. The gas had gone bad ages ago so we were screwed. I don't know why the lodge didn't have solar because that was the law. Maybe because it was only open in the wintertime and because there's so little daylight that time of year… who knows? All we know is that we'll have to move on to a better situation before it gets too cold. We don't have a vehicle so we'll have to hike. We all agreed that we'd stay another two weeks and then we'll move on. Oh well… it was pretty good while it lasted.

There's still a lot of food left in the pantry, but I have to say that we're getting pretty sick of all the canned stuff. Mike's a really good cook and he knows how to make bread and noodles, but he needs water to work his magic, and now that the electric pump doesn't work we have to get water from this stream that's about a mile away. It has to be boiled before we can cook with it, and it's such a pain in the ass hauling those five gallon buckets back and forth, but then Wendy found a wagon in one of the outbuildings with these giant, inflatable wheels so that makes hauling the water a lot easier. We all agreed that she deserved employee of the month over pasta and mandarin oranges the night she found the wagon.

We talked about horses and whether or not it would be practical to use them for riding and farming and what not. Since the local grid had apparently gone down, electric vehicles in the vicinity will be useless, and after a while the solar arrays and wind turbines will stop working because they'll need upkeep, and until we learn how to fix and maintain them we'll be screwed. We also reasoned that a lot of the horses on the ranches might still be cool with being ridden, but we agree that attempting to ride them will be taking a big chance. Margaret worries that if one of us gets thrown or trampled, and because there are literally no more doctors, an injury could be life-threatening. Donny smirked and told us that horses don't want to hurt anyone, but that like any organism, they'll defend themselves. He said that when it came to horses, patience and respect are the key things. He'd grown up on a ranch and told us not to worry. He's good with horses.

Donny and I set out early this morning with full backpacks for a long trek with the intent of finding horses, and preferably ones that had already been broken. We hope to find some that had been turned out prior to second Pollen, and that they'd survived on their own over the last couple of months. Our plan is to get to State Road 93 then head south toward Missoula. Donny knows of a bunch of ranches along 93, and hopefully we'll have some luck. We have some rough country to hike through before we reach the road. If we come across any abandoned vehicles, electric or hydrogen, that will make things that much easier. Wendy gave me her .44 Mag but I didn't tell Donny. He hates guns which is funny for someone who grew up on a ranch. I hate them too, but who knows what we'll run into?

It's now late afternoon. Tomorrow we'll turn off the access road and head south into the woods. This will lob two days off our hike toward 93."

<u>Woodie Epps, 19</u>
<u>Post-Pollen Male</u>
<u>Detroit, Michigan</u>

<u>October, 2089</u>

"I walked into the museum today. I hadn't been there in years. What a change. There was a lot of broken glass on the floor, and a stream of water ran down one of the walls of the Rivera Court. A big chunk of one of the frescos had broken off and lay on the floor like pieces of a puzzle.

My grandmother used to bring me here and she'd say that maybe all these works of art don't mean much now, but they will. This place is holy and good for your soul. She knew all the names of the paintings and told me stories about her favorites. I just listened to her and took it all in, and even though I didn't know what she was talking about half the time, I knew that what she was saying was important. Her words come back to me in dreams sometimes. I walked into her favorite gallery – a small, six-sided room with a dome ceiling, with the walls painted a dark, royal blue and gold trim. Every time we walked into it she'd say it was like walking into a jewelry box. There was a dead, skeletal pit bull lying in the middle of the floor, and a beam of light shone down on it from the skylight above. Funny… outside it would have been just another dead dog lying in the gutter, but here it looked like a work of art.

I was surprised to find that a lot of the paintings still hung on the walls and had not been looted. Some of them were moldy though, and others had been slashed with knives, and a lot of them lay on the floor, their frames bent and broken. This was the work of the pre-Pollen militias. We beat them back and after that they knew better than to come to Detroit and stir up their shit.

Another gallery was filled with paintings of the Madonna and Child, and another had lots of paintings of babies with their parents. I was a baby at one time too, but memories from that far back are vague shadows. The babies in these paintings look so strange and doughy; chubby little things with big, bald heads. They must have been funny looking in real life. I forget what they sounded like.

A lot of the Greek and Roman statues had been knocked over and lay shattered on the floor. I walked back into the Rivera Court and picked up a piece of fresco about the size of a dinner plate. There was a hand holding a wrench painted on it. Maybe my grandmother would say that that hand means that we've got work to do, and she would have been right. I went to school and learned how to read and write. I got the basics down in math and algebra, and although calculus was hard, I passed. I enjoyed history and the humanities, but all that's been wiped away. Christopher Columbus in 1492 doesn't mean a goddamn thing today. It might as well have never happened because everyone who taught us these things is dead and turned to dust. It's only us now – the post-Pollens, and what have we got to offer? What's our contribution? How are we going to change the world? What will we build, and how will we do it? I look around at this old building, with its columns and arches, and vast spaces, with all this art and I don't know where to begin. I don't know what to think, and I have to ask myself, *How did they do this?* Then I looked at my chunk of fresco with the hand holding the wrench, and it dawned on me: There's a library across the street. There are books in there."

Darcy Tindall, 19
Excerpts from an Interview
Broadcast over Multiple Platforms
Medicine Hat, Alberta

Q: What was Oumuamua then, if it wasn't just an asteroid?

Darcy: It was an extraterrestrial object of intelligent origin, and its purpose was to listen and observe in order to detect life on planets throughout the universe. There are millions of these scouts all over the Milky Way Galaxy.

Q: Why?

Darcy: Human DNA can be found on virtually every asteroid and comet in the universe. No one knows its origins. When these asteroids and comets crash into planets where conditions for life are favorable, the DNA evolves. But this DNA, that's to say, the DNA of the pre-Pollen population, was flawed.

Q: How so?

Darcy: Once fully evolved, instead of living in harmony and symbiosis on their host planets, they become viral parasites in every sense of the word. Unchecked, they multiply into the billions and become the dominant species. Their appetites are beyond voracious. Their impact becomes detrimental to the point of mass extinctions of all other living species. Eventually conditions for life are erased and every living organism on the planet dies, all of which can be traced to the activities of the invasive and parasitic human DNA. Those who sent Oumuamua regard this phenomenon as unacceptable, and that it happened here on

Earth is not an isolated incident – this is an unfortunate commonality throughout the universe.

Q: And Pollen?

Darcy: Pollen was a correction. It exterminated the parasite and corrected its DNA. We are the result of that correction.

Q: Will we be capable of reproduction one day?

Darcy: It remains to be seen. There's concern that we've been too influenced by the violence and mayhem of the pre-Pollens.

Q: Who did all this? Who's responsible for Pollen and second Pollen?

Darcy: If I had to assign a name to them it would be a combination of corrector, protector, and mentor.

Q: And how could this Oumuamua object have known that Earth was infected with the flawed DNA from so far away?

Darcy: You're asking about technology that is light years more advanced than anything on Earth, but once it was detected and verified, 600 observers were inseminated into the population; they look exactly like humans; they speak all of the languages and are perfectly assimilated.

Q: Observers? Have you ever met one?

Darcy: Yes, and so have you… in fact you're talking to one right now.

EPILOGUE

Dear Johnathon Jerome Quinn,

I'm adding an epilogue to this book which you assembled with such love and care. I only wish that you could read what I've written here on its last page, but three hundred years have passed since you placed this book on your table. Your bones too, still lay undisturbed in your bed not ten feet from where I now sit. We thank you for the many clues you left behind that finally led us to this home that was clearly built to withstand the vagaries of time.

First, I must state that your name has long been known to us. Our historian was conducting research on our ancestors, the survivors of the *USS Michigan*, and came upon a slip of paper that had been placed in the pages of a library book about submarine warfare. This slip read, "Lieutenant J. J. Quinn, USS Michigan, 10S GJ 06832 44683." We were finally able to decipher the strange combination of numbers and letters after many days of research, and it was this stroke of luck that ultimately led us to you and your book.

Like you, our ancestors were crew members on that submarine where you woke up alone all those years ago. They were the doctors, nurses, and orderlies who kept watch over you as you lay unconscious in the submarine's infirmary. When Pollen occurred, the head surgeon rushed her staff into the sealed quarantine room and there they remained with you for its duration, and like you, they were not exposed to, nor infected with its horrors.

A mass hysteria quickly broke out all over the submarine and the crew of both officers and enlisted personnel were suddenly stricken with an intense claustrophobia brought on by Pollen. The Captain himself took the controls and steered his craft shoreward at full throttle. A couple hundred yards before impact he cut power and the submarine's nose buried itself into that remote beach. The panic and hysteria by then was so intense that the crew immediately and carelessly abandoned ship without protective gear or provisions. The head surgeon and her staff remained in quarantine with you for a time until she deemed it safe to exit. A couple of days transpired then she finally gave the all clear. The medical staff then abandoned ship to conduct a search and rescue. None of the submariners stricken by Pollen survived. The head surgeon and her staff did all they could to save their fellow submariners, but to no avail. Records are sparse, but we believe that all infected hands died of shock and exposure.

You may have thought that the decision to leave you completely alone in the submarine's infirmary to have been a cruel one, but according to the diary of the head surgeon, Lieutenant Commander M. Patricia Grinnell, you had been left behind because you would have died within minutes had you been disconnected from the life-support system. As it turned out, it was the correct decision because you did survive and go on to live an important and meaningful life. When you finally left the submarine, you walked southward, but our ancestors headed north (before you woke from your coma), and that is why your paths never crossed. Three-hundred years have come and gone and we, the descendants of the medical staff of the *USS Michigan,* have finally found you. The circle has closed. Songs will be written and sung in your honor, and you will now take your place in our temple of honored mothers and fathers.

Your book will be read, remembered, and revered, for it tells the story of humans, our extermination, and transformation – a transformation that ultimately failed, for not a single post-Pollen human has lived to see the day on which on I write this epilogue.

We have persevered, but we are small in number. Our survival is not assured. We suffer many hardships brought on by disease and starvation, and too much of the medical knowledge of our ancestors has been lost to the ages. We know the importance of language, and we cherish the words and stories that we find in books throughout the land. It is because of your book that we know of Oumuamua and Pollen – the name for what it brought. We do not want this to happen again.

We are good to the Earth, and please know that our children are brought up to honor and love all living organisms with whom we share it.

Signed on this Day, August 30th, 2393,
With Great Admiration, Love, and Respect-

The Descendants of the Survivors of the
USS Michigan, SSGN-727

AN INDEX OF THE CHRONICLED

Johnathon Jerome Quinn: Chronicler and Assembler of the Book

Dr. Deborah Bernstein: B: 2026 D: 2089 – Chicago, Illinois (Research Scientist) 63
Entries taken from the archives of Dr. Deborah Bernstein housed at the University of Chicago Library, Chicago, Illinois

Jeanette DeLuca: B: 2051 D: 2089 – Marion, Ohio (Teacher) 38
Entry taken from personal papers and notes found in a box in a home in Marion, Ohio

Matthew Delvin: B: 2021 D: 2089 – Los Angeles, California (Hollywood writer) 68
Entries taken from a personal, handwritten diary found in a home in Ventura, California

Woodie Epps: B: 2070 D:_____- Detroit, Michigan. (Post-Pollen Male)
Entry taken from a Q-Hand found in a house in the Boston-Edison neighborhood of Detroit, Michigan

Gregory Felcynn: B 2034 D: 2089 – Washington D.C. (U.S. Census Bureau) 55
Entries taken from the Civil Servant Archive of the Georgetown University Library, Washington D.C.

Reverend Mark D. Hopper: B: 2020 D: 2089 – Charlotte, North Carolina (Evangelical leader) 69
Entries taken from *The Notes and Speeches of the Rev. Mark D. Hopper* found in the archives at the Lockwood Evangelical Church, Charlotte, North Carolina

Dr. Robert Kindler: B: 1995 D: 2082 – Ann Arbor, Michigan (Former Director, CDC) 87
Entries taken from the personal papers of Dr. Robert Kindler, housed at the University of Michigan, Ann Arbor, Michigan

Dawn Leonard: B: 2070 D:_____- Reed, Oklahoma (Post-Pollen Female)
Entries taken from a handwritten diary found in Magnum, Oklahoma

Andy Lerche: B: 2070 D:____ - Sheridan, Wyoming (Post-Pollen Male)
Entries taken from a Q-Hand found in a forest in northern Montana

Dr. Ellitha Mais-Jackson: B: 2019 D: 2089 – Detroit, Michigan (Director, Detroit Institute of Arts) 70
Entry taken from the archives of the Detroit Institute of Arts, Detroit, Michigan

Kendall McClellan: B: 2017 D: 2089 Washington D.C. (United States Senator, Kentucky (R)
Entry taken from the archives of the Honorable Kendall McClellan at the University of Kentucky, Lexington, Kentucky

Phillip Meijerson: B: 2070 D: _____ – Duluth, Minnesota (Post-Pollen Male)
Entries taken from a Q-Hand found in a house in Duluth, Minnesota

Edwin Mossbauer: B: 2050 D: 2089 – Charleston, South Carolina (Motivational Speaker) 39
Entry taken from a personal, handwritten diary found in a house in Charleston, South Carolina

Julia Petyrkowski: B: 2070 D:_____ - Augusta, Maine (Post-Pollen Female)
Entries taken from a Q-Hand found in a house in Augusta, Maine

John Radner: B: 2052 D: 2087 – Kokomo, Indiana (Activist/Conspiracy theorist) 35
Entries from a personal, handwritten journal found in a wooded area 5 miles north of Kearney, Nebraska

Darcy Tindall: B: 2070 D:_____ - Kearney, Nebraska & Medicine Hat, Alberta (Observer)
Transcript of an interview broadcast over multiple platforms

Rebecca Tindall: B: 2054 D: 2089 – Kearney, Nebraska (Mother) 35
Entries taken from a handwritten diary found in a refugee camp near Medicine Hat, Alberta

Paige Vanderzahne: B: 2025 D: 2089 – Dallas (Bluffview) Texas (Bon Vivant) 62
Entry taken from a Q-Hand found in a house in the Bluffview neighborhood of Dallas, Texas

THE BRIGHT AND DARKENED LANDS OF THE EARTH

BY

DONALD LEVIN

On the last day of the world
I would want to plant a tree
--W.S. Merwin, "Place"

PART 1

The First Journey

1

A figure appears in an empty window frame halfway up the ruined wall. Dark glasses on a face wrapped with rags and shaded beneath a hood stare down at her.

The long barrel of a gun points in her direction.

Caught completely out in the open, she has no time to do anything except dive to the ground. She tries to merge with the rubble, disappear into it, though she knows she can't; she is completely exposed. She holds her breath, waiting for the kill shot. She had thought there were no bullets left anymore, but she doesn't want to take any chances.

When the kill shot doesn't come, she dares to lift her head. The window frame is empty.

She scrambles to her feet and turns to flee.

Before going ten feet, she comes face-to-face with the hooded figure holding his rifle.

"Halt!" the figure rasps. The voice is muffled by layers of rags wrapped around its head beneath the hood. But there is no mistaking the rough, deep sound.

It is a raggedman's voice.

She falls to her knees and raises trembling hands.

2

Her day started hours earlier, when the wary young woman—whose name is Ash—picked her way through the debris near the entrance to her underground settlement.

With a staff for balance and protection, she stepped over concrete blocks and ragged piles of broken bricks under the heat of the unrelenting sun. Several times she tripped over planks of charred wood from buildings that had been destroyed in the old wars, concealed under the red dust that coats the land.

Her destination was a few klicks away from their settlement. Wreckage like what surrounded the underground opening was everywhere along the meandering path she traveled. They were taught to avoid moving in a straight line to present less of a target, and also to increase the chances of scavenging valuables buried away from the common paths.

The woman stumbled over the detritus of what was left of the city. She wore a tattered drab coat wrapped around her despite the heat, and she protected her head with an ancient battered welder's helmet that was the unit's only armor against the brilliantly bright, deadly rays of the sun. This was one among a cache of similar helmets that had been scavenged over the years. Nobody knew what they were at first, but when the tribe discovered the helmets' uses, they became treasured finds.

She walked carefully, alert to every movement around her. No animals or insects survived anymore, so chances were any movement would be hostile. The only sound was the wind soughing against the metal of her helmet. She swiveled her head constantly. The helmet restricted her view, but its protection against the damaging rays of the sun outweighed any limitations to her vision.

Ash walked over the streets, cracked and overgrown with the skeletal remains of trees and bushes. No one could remember the last time it had rained, not even the elders; plant life had turned brown and desiccated in the absence of water, disappearing like the animals.

Her destination rose ahead of her. It was a larger building than most in the area, originally three stories tall. One entire wall had fallen over in the tremor that rolled through the land the day before.

After a collapse was the worst time to be out scavenging. The dangers from old structures were multiplied after one toppled; the ground grows unsteady around them, so the ones nearby are liable to let go and fall, too. The mortar between blocks is dry, the ruined buildings unstable.

Their original purposes have been lost, but their current usefulness sometimes surprises the survivors who venture from their underground settlement to scavenge. While most such buildings, like the one Ash sought, had long been emptied of any water or food, they sometimes yielded tools or pieces of clothing or other prizes that made exploring them worth the danger. Especially after a collapse, which often uncovered treasures previously hidden to the Vengers who searched.

Ash is a Venger. When Vengers found objects that might be of use, they would bring them back to the settlement. If they found potential food sources, they were to return and inform their work unit's leader, who would let the Vesters know. They, in turn, would go out and harvest the food. The practice had developed to ensure their survival, and so far it was working, if barely; Ash's settlement was on the verge of starvation.

Slowly the food sources have been dwindling. As they did, so too did the tribe. The Vengers had to travel further and further from their underground settlement to find food, and sometimes they returned empty-handed and sometimes they did not return at all.

Ash paused when she was about a half-klick away from the structure she sought. She scanned the site through the dark glass of her helmet. Then, stepping carefully while still some distance away, she circled the ruin once, twice, three times, all the while keeping watch for anything moving in the wreckage. It wouldn't take much to overwhelm her; one raggedman alone could do it if he caught her by surprise.

On her third circuit around the building, a sound reached her, penetrating her helmet. It was high and keening. Though she had not heard a baby cry in years, this brought back the sound of an infant's mewl. Of course that would be impossible; few children have been born in the recent past. And no child would have survived for long in the outside.

She stopped, knelt low, and listened. The crying ceased, but then she heard what she thought was pounding. She raised the faceplate of her helmet, aware as she did that she was allowing the deadly radiation inside the metal. But she needed to find out what the sound was.

She lifted her head, with the helmet guard ajar so she could see into the shadows that surrounded the building. She listened but heard no more wailing.

Then she heard a scratching and scrambling in the rubble. She stood perfectly still, aware that she was unprotected outside the ruins of the building.

And that this might be a trap.

Then she looked up and saw the figure with the long gun in the empty window frame.

3

"Who are you?" the raggedman now demands. He shoves the rifle barrel at her, emphasizing his impatience.

She is too scared to reply. She has heard stories about encounters like these, but has never had one herself. It is a rule never to engage with the raggedmen they see during their scavenging. In her settlement, others who had been in the Upground more than she had told stories of meeting raggedmen out there. Most of them were veterans of either the Large War or the endless smaller skirmishes over food and water and other resources that claimed the lives of so many, prompting the social breakdown that followed—massive die-offs of populations, riots, the final deterioration of the environment.

Enough Vengers had returned to the home area with tales of having escaped violent encounters with these old vets to justify being cautious—and to strike fear within her. These encounters never ended well.

He looks around as though expecting someone to come after him. What have I wandered into, she wonders. Are there more raggedmen around?

Most importantly, how can I get away, with this pointed at me? There aren't many of these old weapons left, but she has seen the damage they could do in the torn and bloody flesh of the men whom the Vesters bring back to their underground home.

"Alone?" he asks.

She nods.

He raises the rifle barrel, indicating she should stand. She gets to her feet and stands on watery legs. He points the rifle toward an opening in the wall behind her. "Go," he says.

She shakes her head.

"Go!"

"No!"

He takes a step toward her and with the gun barrel pushes her roughly toward the opening, then into a chamber formed by collapsed cinder blocks. The roof of the ruined building is gone, but only spots of sunlight penetrate the area, dappling the scattered bricks and splintered wood and rotted planks. A slab of fallen wall angles overhead and keeps most of the room in shadow. With the tinted glass of her helmet, she is almost blind.

A final shove with the rifle knocks her to her knees. She pulls her helmet off and crawls away from him into a corner.

At least she can see better now. Though she sees no escape for herself.

The man looks around one more time, then leans the rifle against the side of the chamber and bends to twist her onto her back. Instinctively, she covers her body and braces for whatever is to come.

But all he wants is the plastic container than hangs from her belt. Her water. He grabs it from her and downs the entire contents in three gulps.

"More?" he asks.

She shakes her head. "Done."

He tosses the container at her and looks her over.

"You have?" he asks.

"Done," she repeats, thinking he is talking about the water. "No more."

"YOU HAVE?" he roars.

"No more!"

He pulls at her clothes. He rips open her coat and feels around her body with rough hands. He flips her onto her stomach and she feels his hands grabbing at her shoulders, between her legs, down her thighs and calves to her feet.

When he finishes, he flips her again so she is on her back, looking up at him.

"You don't have it," he mutters, as though to himself. "You were telling the truth."

The sudden expansion of his language from the sparse style most people use surprises her. The chief elder of her tribe uses language like this in her songs; Ash recognizes it.

Over the decades, the once-supple instrument of spoken language has been pared down to the point where few words are ever used for anything, except formal ceremonial occasions with the tribe, when the chief elder, as Singer, sings her songs. Ash understands more than she can express, but both comprehension and expression are limited in her world.

Still, she tries to match his language. "There is no more water." she says slowly.

"Water?" He waves that away and says, "Nay. I mean the book."

She looks at him in confusion, and he repeats, "The book!"

"What is 'the book'?"

He watches her, as though trying to decide if she is kidding or not. "You don't know?" he asks.

She shakes her head.

As if all the air goes out of him, he falls back onto the ruined blocks and puts his face against his knees. He covers his head with his hands and makes the high whining sound like an infant's cry she heard a few minutes earlier. That a raggedman could make such a sound confuses her.

Then he says, "So you're not looking for it?"

She shakes her head. "Venger," she says, pointing to herself. "Look for anything tribe can use."

"But not a book?"

She shrugs to indicate her lack of understanding.

He shakes his head. "The book is here," he says. "Somewhere."

"What is a 'book'?" she asks again.

In response, he begins to wheeze, a heavy sound like a bag of wet sand shifting in his chest. She can't tell if he is laughing at her until he begins to gasp for air and she knows he's not joking.

Still, this is a raggedman. And she has just met him. She doesn't know his real intention; all she knows are the typical intentions of men.

She leaps up and runs toward the entrance to the chamber. Quicker than she would have thought possible, he dives for her and grabs her ankle as she rushes past and she falls heavily against the ragged stone wall. She cries in pain and feels her cheek go numb. A wound scrapes open on the side of her face where she falls.

"Wait," the man gasps. He grabs her by the other ankle.

She kicks wildly at the hands that hold her. "Wait!" he says again. She can feel his strength fading and she scrambles out of his grasp and up onto her hands and knees. She looks around the rubble-strewn chamber for something to hit him with. She grabs a length of wood and jumps up, ready to swing at him.

In the struggle with her, the wrapping has come loose from around his head. The sight of his face makes her pause with the wood in her hand. The skin is raw and blistered from exposure to the sun, with the lumpy thickening of the skin typical of veterans exposed to the poisons of the wars. Straggly patches are all that are left of his hair. She has seen it before in men whom the Vesters led into their settlement, but she has never seen it this close-up.

Fascinated and repulsed, she examines his twisted face and raw head. He must be in agony.

He holds his hands up in supplication. "Please. Please."

"Sick?" she asks.

"Aye."

"Drag up soon?"

Now it's his turn to shake his head. He does not understand the phrase.

She drops the length of wood and stands over him. He is not a threat, she decides. Not in this condition.

"Die soon," she translates.

He nods.

"Name, you?" she asks.

"Jo."

She nods, points to herself and says, "Ash."

"The book," he says, "is here. Somewhere." He gestures around him.

"What is 'book'?" she asks for the third time.

Before answering, he stifles a coughing attack. Then, his hacking finished, he parts his coat to reveal a small pack tied around his waist. Carefully he withdraws a small pliable thing that is about the size of his hand. It is grey with age and dirt. He holds it up to her. "This," he says, "is a book." She reaches out for it, but he pulls it away—"Please, don't touch"—and replaces it in his pack. "Delicate. Not many left anymore. Most rotted away years ago. In the ruins of this stinking civilization."

"How do you know?" she asks.

"About the book?"

She nods.

"I've been looking for a long time. It's been a rumor for years that it's out here. A few of us look. They didn't get us all in the Purge."

Ash again doesn't know what that means.

"The Great Purge during the war?" he asks.

She shrugs.

"They tried to get rid of anyone who could read. They couldn't get all of us."

She has not heard about this. Knowledge, especially of history, is only what she knows from the Singer's songs, and they have not touched on anything called The Great Purge.

"One of the rumors was," Jo went on, "that the book might be here. In this school. Left over from the beforetime."

"School?" she asks. Another unfamiliar word.

A coughing fit doubles him over. She wishes she had water to give him, but he drank all of hers.

"You have book," she says. She points at the place under his coat where she saw his pack. "Why need two?"

He taps his pack beneath his coat and says, "This book is old. Poetry. Poetry? You know poetry? Poems?"

She shakes her head.

"Have you heard songs in your tribe? There's a Singer?"

Ash nods. "Singer makes songs."

"Songs are poetry. A kind of poetry, anyway." The look of confusion on Ash's face makes him say, "It's no matter. The book I'm looking for is different. It's not as old as the poetry. It tells the story of all this." He moves his hands in the air, describing what seem to be mysterious clouds or smoke. "It predicts how it came to this. It tells about the end."

"The end?"

"It says how everything will end. Society, culture . . . the world our ancestors made. And then destroyed."

She follows his words with difficulty.

"The legend is, the book was right about how it all would end. So there might be something in it about how we can go on. Some clue about how to at least survive this nightmare we've created."

Who was "we"? She had never seen this raggedman before. And anyway, how could a book tell their story? How could they change their end? Her tribe could barely survive from day to day, let alone have any effect on how they lived.

Ash thinks about that, then shakes her head. This is getting beyond her.

"You find the book," he says. "I'll tell you what's in it."

"You read?"

"I read."

"But you raggedman?"

In her experience, all the men in this world are raggedmen. Men who survived the wars, the lethal sunlight, the lack of food or water, and the radiation, and who continue to survive by preying on anyone they met, including women and other raggedmen. There were some raggedwomen in the Upground, but not many. And none of them know anything about reading or books.

Killing, aye. They know much about killing.

"Only look like a raggedman," he says with a weak smile. "Friend. Trying to keep an old tradition alive."

He starts to get up, but he is too weak and collapses back to the ground with more coughing. "Help me," he says. "Find the book. Please."

"I don't know what a book is," she says.

"I'll tell you. Then you can find it."

4

As best he can, he tells her where she might look for this thing called a book. He shows her his book again, then clears a space on the ground and with his finger draws a rudimentary picture of the thing in the sand so she will know how it is different from his book.

She leaves him propped against the inside wall and picks her way through the remains of the building. He has made her understand that she should look for the book on every level, but she finds there are no full levels left, just three walls of the building's shell and sections of floors leading up to the top. The rest has collapsed; she remembers this is her reason for being here, to search the ruins for anything usable.

Leaving her welder's helmet on the ground beside him, she goes out into the large area that completes the first floor of the building and clambers up a mound of dirt and concrete as high as she can go. Then she hauls herself up to the second level using whatever hand- and footholds in the walls she can find. She pauses there to catch her breath. Only a path hugging the walls is left of the floor.

By this method, she climbs to the top level. There, more of the flooring is left, enough floorspace to support small rooms lining the three remaining walls.

She searches through each room, carefully sorting through the building's rubble with her hands and her staff. In the fourth room, she finds something that looks like the diagram the man drew in the sand. It is shaped like the book he carries with him, but much larger and thinner, made out of hard metal. On it are markings and images she cannot decipher; she supposes that understanding those marks is what people meant by "reading." She has never learned; it is a skill that has all but disappeared in her world. She doubts if anyone in her tribe knows how, even the chief elder.

She tucks the thing into the waistband of her pants and continues searching through the remaining rooms, then goes down to the next level and keeps searching.

But she finds nothing else that looks like what the man described, nor anything else that might be useful to her tribe. Hoping she is bringing back the correct thing, she makes her way down to the ground, to the chamber where she left the man Jo.

When she gets there, she discovers he has toppled over from the sitting position where she left him. Thinking he has passed out, she approaches him and tries to help him back to a sitting position. She calls his name: "Jo?"

Instead, he falls over onto his other side. Her hands come away from him soaked with blood.

They are behind her.

Two of them.

Their faces are covered, wrapped in rags like everything else in this world, but they are men. She can tell from their size and the way they move, and their smell, the man-stench that makes her gag.

They must be practiced hunters because they move in on her, one on each side, without communication between them. One of them holds the rifle that Jo had pointed at her. The other holds a long knife. Even in the shadows of the chamber, she can tell that it is red with blood.

Jo's blood.

Neither raggedman says anything, but one of them makes a low growl.

In an instant they charge her. She parries the knife with her staff. The man holding the gun swings it like a club and she tries to block it but can't and it connects with the side of her head. The world explodes in flashes of bright light and then just as suddenly goes dark.

5

She comes to lying on her back. One of the men is kneeling over her and pawing at her clothes as he tries to tear them off. She has heard from others about the dangers of being taken by raggedmen—the violence of it, the raw, painful burning of its aftermath.

No, she thinks in panic, this will not happen. Before she can move, she is overcome by a wave of nausea and vomits in the face of the man above her. The surprise of it stops him for a moment. She begins to flail, kicking her legs and swinging her arms wildly.

Her staff is nowhere near, but the man is no match for her thrashing. She kicks him off and pushes him away and sends a foot into his face.

The other man, the one with the knife, raises it menacingly but she scrambles to her feet and scoops up whatever she can pick up in her hands from the floor—dust and small rocks—and throws it in his eyes. It blinds him and stops him long enough to allow her to grab her staff and she is about to run him through with it but he turns and blunders, still half-blinded, out of the chamber.

She notices the other man has already left out another doorway.

She falls backward and hits the ground heavily beside Jo's body. Her head feels as if it has been split open as she tries to stand, not wanting to be caught on the ground again if the two men decide to return.

She vomits and lies back down. She vomits again.

The men had torn off her clothes, everything except for the coat, and scattered them around the chamber. She tries to feel if they have attacked her anywhere else beside her head. She feels between her legs . . . no, she came around before they could take her.

Fighting more nausea, willing herself not to think, she crawls over the debris on the floor and collects her clothes. Slowly, painfully, she climbs back into them.

And then remembers: the book!

She looks around. Where is it?

She sees it on the other side of the chamber. Unsteadily, she struggles to her feet, her head pounding and nausea again gripping her. She bends over but only gags; she has nothing left to bring up.

She retrieves the book. She recognizes the scratching on it, so she is certain it is what she found on the upper level. Except the metal case has been opened and it is torn in half at the hinge, the two parts left on the floor. One half of the inside is smooth, and the other has small buttons with indecipherable symbols on each.

She joins the two pieces and replaces the thing where she had carried it, at her waist. She steadies herself and eases over to the entrance to look outside. No sight of the men, or anyone else.

She can tell by the quality of the light that it is evening, almost full night. She does not know that the sun never sets, continuing to bathe the ground with UV radiation unimpeded by the thinning atmosphere, because she is so high north, near what used to be Thompson, Manitoba, in Canada; all she knows is that the light from the sun at night is different from the day, milkier, less intense.

She is afraid to make the trip back to the settlement now. She is too shaky, and too afraid of who else she might meet.

She goes back inside the chamber where the dead man is. She collects large pieces of debris to cover him—boards and blocks—and pulls some over herself in case of visitors.

Holding her staff, she spends the rest of the night beside Jo. She tries to stay awake and vigilant, but at some point she falls asleep.

6

In the morning, she wakes with her joints stiff and her head even more painful than the day before. The dead man is beginning to smell in the heat. She stands shakily; her legs tremble, her vision blurs, and nausea overcomes her. When she is certain she isn't going to dry heave again, she searches through the dead man's clothes to see if he has anything she can use. There is nothing, not even a knife.

The pack where he kept his poetry book is gone. She looks around but doesn't see it. The two men who killed him must have taken it.

After first making sure no one is outside, she struggles to fit the welder's helmet onto her aching head, then climbs out of the chamber into the blazing morning heat and begins the trek home.

Mostly women live in their settlement, with a few old men who had been too old or too sick to fight in the wars. Together, they all survive in the underground network of tunnels that had once been a nickel mine in the Before.

How long ago the Before was, few knew anymore. Such wisdom resided with the chief elder, whose responsibility it was not only to lead the Council of Elders and therefore the tribe, but also to keep the legends alive and handed down, and to sing about them in the traditional songs to remind the tribe where they came from.

Where they are going is not so important; no one knows. The word "tomorrow" has passed from their vocabulary; life for them is a day-to-day struggle; the future has no meaning.

The guard at the entrance to the settlement knows something is wrong as soon as Ash draws near, stumbling and weaving over the bricks and blocks. The guard calls for assistance, but Ash has passed out by the time they carry her down the mine entrance and through the narrow tunnels to the room she shares with five other Vengers.

She sleeps for a day and a night.

She has familiar dreams . . . of herself as a child, dirty and hungry, the product of a single violent encounter between an unknown raggedman and the woman who lies sprawled beside the infant girl, the woman's fevered, delusional screams now silenced forever . . . of the unforgiving sun baking down, burning the skin of the child who has no understanding of the need to hide from it in the Upground wasteland where they have been wandering, the only life the child knows . . . of the two women, Vengers, who find the child and take her back to their underground dwelling . . . of the dark, suffocating world where she will spend the rest of her days, with occasional forays into the light . . .

When Ash wakes, her work unit leader is next to her pallet on the floor.

Ash sits up, startled, then the pain in her head compels her to lie down again.

The team leader says nothing.

After a while, Ash searches on the floor around her.

"What you brought?" the team leader asks.

Ash nods.

"Safe."

"Where?"

"Elders have it."

Ash's look of confusion and upset prompts the leader to say, "Safe. Worry not. And you?"

Ash takes stock of how she feels. Her head is still painful and she is sore all over. But she is glad to be back in the settlement.

"Raggedmen take you?" her leader asks. *Take* is the euphemism for rape.

"Try. But nay."

The unit leader nods. This, Ash knows, is both good and bad. Good, because being taken is a harsh and terrible act, and more women dragged up in childbirth than lived.

Bad because this is how the tribe continues. Without occasional impregnation by the raggedmen, the group will fade out as the women and old men grow old and drag up. It is best if the act is done in the safe confines of the settlement, and not in the world, where being taken can be fatal.

Ash puts a hand to her head to steady the world from spinning, then gathers herself to stand.

"Nay," the unit leader says. "Stay."

"Work?" Ash knows if she doesn't work, she won't eat.

"Nay work. Stay."

The unit leader stands and leaves the cell.

Ash falls back to sleep.

This time her sleep is dark and empty.

7

The Council of elders sit in a semi-circle on the ground in their Council chambers. Nine women, old, lean, with the shrunken, waxy pallor of starvation and lack of sunlight. The oldest is the chief elder, sitting cross-legged at the head of the semi-circle. She is called Odile. It is thought among the tribe that she remembers the Before, but nobody knows how old that would make her, or indeed even when the Before was; it exists now as a mythical state out of time and history, recreated for the tribe only in the chief elder's songs.

Like the other women, Odile is wrapped in tattered clothing, but curled around locks of her hair are dead twigs, a sort of dried laurel wreath made from what is left of the sprawling evergreen forests of the Before.

Ash stands in the Council chamber in the center of the semi-circle. She has never been here before. Workers of her station are not allowed here. She does not look at the elders in the flickering torch light—that would be too brazen—but at the thing she had brought back with her from her travels. It is in front of the chief, broken in two, as it was when she found it after she fought off the men in the chamber of the collapsed building.

The chief elder says, "Ash."

Ash looks up but cannot maintain eye contact with so important a member of their tribe.

"You found this?" the chief elder asks, indicating the object in front of her.

Ash nods. "A book," she offers, hoping to impress them with her knowledge.

But the chief elder shakes her head. "Nay. Nay book."

Ash looks at the two pieces of metal, then back at the elder. "Nay book?"

The elder shakes her head again, this time with sadness.

"But—" Ash begins. It must be the right one, she thinks, but realizes she has no way of knowing if it is or not. The man Jo asked her to find it, but she never got to show it to him because he was dead by the time she returned to him.

Besides, who is she to argue with the chief elder?

"Nay book," the elder says. "This is a machine."

Machine. The word is unfamiliar to Ash.

"A tool," the chief elder says when she sees Ash does not understand. "Broken, but a tool all the same."

Then the chief elder asks, "Why did you think this was a 'book'?"

Ash searches for words to explain. But the words don't come. All she can come up with is "School," the word the dead man had used. She doesn't know what it means, but it seemed to have power for him, and he used it in connection with the book he wanted her to find.

It gets the attention of Odile, who repeats the word, then thinks about it.

"How do you know it was a school?" Odile asks.

"Man say," Ash continues.

"Man?" Odile says. "What man?"

"Man I meet at school. Tell me about the book."

Odile looks at the other elders, then back at Ash.

From within her robes, the chief elder removes a flat piece of paper that has been folded many times. She carefully unfolds a large ragged green and blue sheet in the center of the circle of elders. The paper has markings on it inside shapes of colors.

Odile puts a finger on one set of markings and taps it. "School," she says. Ash still does not know what a school is.

THE BRIGHT AND DARKENED LANDS

Odile seems to intuit Ash's lack of comprehension. "*School.* Place of books," she says. "Place of wisdom. Here is the school where you found the machine," Odile says, tapping the spot on the map.

Odile sits back. "Did the man say what is in the book?" she asks.

Ash struggles to explain, and can only repeat the few words she remembers the man saying. "End. Book tell end." She tries to recapture the flow of words that the man used. "Man say book 'predict end.' He say, if we know, we can change how we end."

"Oh, *man* say," another member of the Council puts in.

The other elders turn to the speaker. The chief elder throws a sharp look at her. She is as old as the others, with the same long matted grey hair, but without the chief elder's laurel branches.

"*Man* say," the woman repeats. "Why do we believe a *man*?"

"Ells," the chief elder says, "let Ash finish."

Ells bristles, but keeps silent.

The chief elder looks toward Ash and nods for her to go on.

"Man say the book would be at the school," Ash says. She has no idea if this were true or not; she still isn't entirely sure what *school* means.

The chief elder follows a blue line on the paper and moves her finger to another set of markings, and taps that. "There is also a school here." She traces a line further up the map. "Here, too. There are many schools."

Ash examines the old woman's wrinkled face for some understanding.

"These are all different places," Odile explains. "Many schools. Maybe the book is in one of them?"

"Or here?" says Ells, the other elder who had spoken up. She flits her hand towards the map, pointing to random locations around it and the room. "Or here? Or there? Or there?"

107

As with most things, Ash does not understand, and knows it is her place not to understand.

Ells shakes her head. "Nay book," she says.

"Must read book," Ash says, remembering finally what the man, Jo, had told her. The elders' heads snap towards Ash, who, suddenly ashamed at speaking up, looks down.

"Who read? *You* read?" Ells asks Ash.

"Nay. Nay read." Ash hopes this admission of her ignorance will pacify the elder.

It does not pacify the elder called Ells. "Book from man," Ells says. "Remember old wise? '*All evil spring from man.*' First rule. Man is evil. The book from man, book evil, too. Nay woman read book, say I."

She looks from one to the other of the elders. Some nod in agreement.

"Council speak," says Ells. "Talk end."

The chief elder says, "Not till I say. And I say nay."

Now the other elders look at her.

"We talk about a *book*!" she says. "We haven't seen a book since when? Never! Here may be a book!" She indicates the map spread out in front of her. "We have a chance to find a relic of the Before!"

"Why?" Ells demands. "Will a book feed us? Protect us? Do *anything* for us? Nay. Tribe nay need book."

"The book may help us," the chief elder says. "Books have wisdom we forget."

"Book is *evil*," says Ells. "From man. Tribe nay need book, say I."

The chief elder stares at her. The other members of the elder's council nod in agreement, except for one.

"The book may help," the lone dissenter appeals to the council. "Let us see the book first, then decide after."

"Agree," the chief elder says.

Ells says, "I say nay. What say council?"

She glares at the other members of the council, daring them to contradict her.

Only two do, the chief elder and the elder who has just spoken up in favor of seeing the book first. One by one, the others say, "Nay book."

Thus denied by the other members of the Council of elders, Odile folds up her map. "Council has spoken, then," she says with sadness. "It is decided. Nay book."

With that, the chief elder stands and looks at each of the other elders. Her eyes come to rest on Ells. "This is a mistake. A foolish mistake."

"*Book* is mistake," Ells spits.

Odile turns and limps out of the chamber. Slowly, giving her time to depart, the others stand and leave in their turn. The one member who had spoken up in favor of the book stays behind. No one dismisses Ash, who still stands in her place, forgotten by them.

The other woman comes near Ash. "Mae," the woman says, pointing to herself. Ash sees that she is younger than the others, though not as young as Ash herself.

"I think the book is important," Mae says. "We need it."

Ash does not know how to respond. There is nothing she can do about any of it. She has never seen a book before, and could not read one if she held it in her hands. She has no say in this matter.

Mae pats Ash's arm, and, without another word, walks out of the elders' chamber and disappears into the tunnels.

Ash bows her head in supplication to the Council, then returns to her work unit for the evening feeding.

8

Noises wake her. The soft scrape of feet on the dirt floor, the rustle of stiff rags.

Ash pops awake to see the chief elder kneeling by her bed. The woman's face looms close as she puts her hand over Ash's mouth before Ash can react.

Odile pulls Ash up from her pallet on the floor and leads her quietly out of the room and down to an empty corridor lit by a low torch. The rest of the workers remain asleep.

Ash sees a bundle on the floor beside a welder's helmet. From out of the shadows steps the woman who called herself Mae.

"You met Mae?" the chief elder asks.

"Aye," Ash says.

Mae gives her a sad smile.

"You go," Odile says in a low voice. "Find the book. Bring it to me."

"But Council say—"

Odile waves Ash's objection away before she can finish it. "The Council is wrong. The book may be more important than they know. If we can find it, we must look at it."

The sudden rush of words reminds Ash of the way Jo spoke at the ruin.

She understands enough of the words to get the chief elder's meaning. "But I disobey—?" she begins. She can't bring herself to finish the sentence. She could be beaten for disobeying the Council in even the smallest matter. For something like this . . . she can't bear to think of it.

The chief elder shakes her head. "Let me worry, not you. You find the book."

Mae hands Ash the bundle from the floor. It is filled with several containers of water, and a pack of strips of the dried meat that is the group's diet. It is tough and hard to chew with the pains in her teeth and gums that plague Ash, along with most of the tribe. But it is all they have to sustain them anymore.

Also in the pack is the folded-up sheet of paper the chief elder had used during the council meeting to show where the schools were. In the dim light of the evening torches, Odile unfolds the map on the floor and points out several locations to Ash.

"We are here. You go this way, follow the path from the entrance. At the river, turn right. Tomorrow, maybe the next day, you'll come to the first school, near where the big water is. Search for the book at the school there. If the book is not at that school, keep this way, with the big water on your right hand." She touches Ash's right hand.

"But work?" Ash says. "Must work. Nay work, nay food. Nay food—?"

"Nay worry. You find the book and bring it back. Give it to me. Only to me. You understand?"

Ash does not understand. A dozen questions and objections fill her mind, primary of which was, Why me?

"Also, here, take this," the chief elder says. She hands Ash a sheet of paper that has a rough shape drawn in charcoal. "The book will look like this. The outside is hard, but the pages inside are soft." She makes a wavering motion with her hands to show Ash that the interior of the book is soft, like the rags that cover their bodies in the wind.

"You see?" Odile asks.

Ash nods.

"Now go," the chief elder says. "While it is night. Take this."

Mae hands Ash a fighting staff of the kind the Vesters use, a long wooden pole with sharpened points on both ends.

"Find the book," the chief elder says. "And bring it back."

PART II

The Second Journey

9

Ash has no trouble locating the river, now as wide as a lake from the backflow from the body of water that used to be called Hudson Bay. In the soft light of early morning, made dimmer by the smoked glass of her helmet, she shuffles through a shallow gully beside the river bed. Here and there she passes the fine, feathery skeletons of long-dead lake creatures peeking through the sand of the gulley, left as the waters of the river have begun to recede. It is as if the world is beginning to contract.

When the day heats up, she pauses to rest. All she can hear in her helmet are the echoes of her own blood beating in her head, and being so exposed worries her. She climbs up the bank and heads toward a hillock of dead trees. There is no shade, but she thinks she can find somewhere safer than being out in the open where she can rest for a while and eat.

She doesn't want to wander too far from the riverbed, so she follows beside it, then, not seeing any possibilities for shelter, she slides back down the bank and continues walking, this time closer to the shore. After a while, she sees an overhang that casts narrow shade where she can get out of the sun. She hunkers down and pulls off her helmet.

She unwraps the package that the chief elder had given her. It holds several days' worth of strips of dried meat. The tribe has long since used up their stores of salvaged canned fruits and vegetables, and agriculture is no longer possible in the dead land. Ash has heard rumors that other tribes in other locations have rediscovered the secret to growing food again, but that's all they are: just rumors.

So they have to satisfy themselves with the meagre portions of meat they eat twice a day. The elders know they are slowly starving, but even Odile, the group's wisest head, does not know how to prevent it. The Vesters bring back many stories of other tribes that have dragged up from starvation or illness, or were slaughtered by others for whatever food they might have been able to provide.

What is left of the human race is slowly going extinct, just as the other species on earth have already done on the dead, toxic, warming planet.

She eats two strips of meat, then, though she is still hungry, she wraps up the rest and stows it in her pack. The familiar thirst gnaws at her; usually the meat they eat has been prepared with more liquid, but the chief elder had given her a ration of dried meat to last through the trip without spoiling. She takes a small sip of water and gathers up her pack and spear. She replaces her helmet and strikes out again.

She walks all day, pausing several more times for a rest. As the heat lessens toward evening, the aches and pains in her legs and blisters on the bottoms of her feet tell her she needs to stop for the night. She finds a small cavern at the side of the bank and looks inside. It smells damp, but is basically dry and, more importantly, empty.

She finds dry brush and sweeps away her footprints from the sand in front of the entrance to the cavern. She crawls inside and pulls the brush across the entrance so no one would know she is there (she hopes). She curls up in the rear of the cavern, and closes her eyes.

She is so tired, she drops off right away.

10

She sleeps until the voices of men wake her.

She can't understand their language, but she thinks she hears three different voices. The low, gruff sounds are unfamiliar to her. It would be three against one if they found her; she would not last long.

They sound like they are right outside her hiding place. Their voices are loud and angry, as men always are when there are more than two of them.

She thinks she hears two of the men moving away. Where is the third?

She hears no further sounds, until the dry branch in front of the cavern begins to rustle.

The man is moving it!

Her stomach lurches. She grabs for her staff at her side. Lying on her back with her feet extended toward the entrance, she tries to make herself as small as possible in the rear of the space while silently extending one of the sharpened points of the spear outward.

She watches the branch moving away, letting more of the night's sunlight penetrate her hideaway. She sees the man's head appear in the opening he is creating. Like the man she had met in the ruined building, this one's head is swaddled in rags, with a dusty bandana tied across his mouth.

The raggedman clears the cavern entrance of brush so he can fit inside. He sticks his head in, and Ash hears his harsh breathing and smells his foul man-smell. Like her, he must be looking for a safe place to spend the night.

He eases himself further inside, crawling on his belly. He doesn't seem to notice her. That is, until he pauses, panting. He happens to raise his head and looks right at Ash.

He catches his breath.

They both stop breathing.

The moment stretches.

Then he takes a sudden gulp of air and his arm shoots out to grab her leg. She is not quick enough and he catches her and holds on. He shouts something.

His voice is loud and dull in the earthen confines of the hiding place.

He reaches out and grabs her other leg. She kicks but he holds on.

He shouts again.

She can't allow him to call a third time. His companions must still be within hearing distance.

She thrusts the sharpened staff toward him. She aims for his eye socket, his most vulnerable part, but misses and drives the point into his forehead. It doesn't pierce the bone but she hears the crack of his neck snapping as the force of her lunge drives his head back.

He collapses where he lies, motionless, half-in and half-out of the cavern.

She grabs under his arms and pulls him all the way inside, then scrambles over him and pulls the dry brush back over the mouth of the little cave. She stays silent and unmoving for several minutes, waiting to see if the others come to help their companion.

She tries to quiet her panting, but cannot. Killing her first man—quickly, without thought—gives her a rush that makes her heart race.

She lies back and peers at him, watching for signs of life. There are none; he had dragged up instantly as soon as his neck broke.

She waits.

His companions do not come to investigate.

She lies watching him for a while longer, then bends forward and begins to unwrap the rags from around his head.

11

In the morning, she makes sure no one is waiting outside the entrance of the cavern, then crawls out. She has wrapped around her own head the rags of the raggedman she killed, and stepped into the pants he wore and the blanket he used as a poncho. She stripped him of his water containers and an ancient can containing what she hopes is food.

She covers up the opening and leaves the dead raggedman there, loosely covered with her own clothes. She leaves her welder's helmet. She resumes her trudge along the river.

Anyone looking at her would assume she is another man walking along the river; the man-smell she carries on her borrowed clothes completes the illusion. Despite the pointless violence that flares between men, it is still safer to walk as a man than as a lone woman.

As she gets closer to the first destination that the chief elder told her about, she is surprised to see so many raggedmen walking in that direction, too. Alone or in twos and threes, converging along with Ash on the remains of the small city near the bay. What could be there that draws them?

And how will she find the school and the missing book?

She walks.

For the most part, the raggedmen are some distance away from the river, so she has little interaction with them. They throw her the occasional distrustful glance, but she ignores them with all the power that dressing in men's clothes gives her.

Once a man jumps out from behind a fallen tree trunk and shouts something at her in a language she doesn't understand. She wonders if raggedmen speak their own language that only they can know, or if it is simply meaningless babble.

This one seems rabid, almost foaming at the mouth, and spits when he yells at her. She tries to ignore him, but he charges toward her.

She braces herself and holds her staff out, ready to fight, and that scares him off. He lets her go on her way and runs after another lone traveler in the distance.

The trip takes two more days. By the time she arrives, she has eaten through her rations of meat and the can she took off the raggedman she killed in the cavern—beans, as it turns out, old and bitter but edible. She still has water in one of the containers she took from him, but she knows she has to save that for the trip back.

If she survives to make the journey.

12

Odile wakes late.

She lies for a while on her pallet in the private chamber she shares with Mae, waiting for the pains in her legs and her back—and, indeed, everywhere—to subside long enough to allow her to begin the laborious task of getting up.

It's not just age that slows her down, she knows; her body is starting to show signs of the sickness that will kill them all, sooner or later. They have no physicians, no medicines, and no knowledge that might allow them to mitigate the suffering, let alone postpone the inevitable.

She has seen her people drag up, one by one, and knows her time will come soon.

She sits up and waits for the sharpest pains to pass before attempting to stand. Mae's pallet is already empty; she must have arisen before Odile.

Odile makes her way down to the sanitation chamber, where she squats over the trench. She nods to the others who are using it. It is particularly ripe today. She will have to remember to speak with the leader of the sanitation group and make sure they give more attention to cleaning this out.

She rinses her hands in a trough of water and makes her way down the tunnel to the feeding chamber. It is still early in the day, but most of the work groups are already out performing their duties, so only a few women linger over their first meals.

Mae is not among them.

The chief feeder greets Odile, and gives her too many strips on the wooden planks that serve as plates. "No," Odile says, as she does every morning, "too many. Too many." She pushes the plank back toward the feeder so the feeder can take some of the strips away. She doesn't need that much food anymore, and she would prefer to save it for the others.

She sits by herself at a bench with her plank of meat and a cup made from a hollowed-out piece of wood from the outside. She sucks the juice from the meat—and it is relatively fresh, so there is still some juice that remains—and washes it down with a drink of water. She has never tasted fresh, clean water; the only water available to them comes from an underground aquifer, and like all the water across the world it is tainted from the wars and pollution from the civilization of which they are the last, dying remnants.

But the water they collect from the underground stream is still cleaner than whatever is available from the outside. The closest water is the river that backflows from the large bay near where Ash is headed, and Odile knows that water is toxic.

She hopes Ash remembers that from her training as a Venger.

Things have gotten worse since Odile was young. Like many women her age, she was orphaned in the food wars that claimed her mother's life while her father was away fighting. In the world she inhabits, most births are the products of encounter between a man whom the Vesters captured and a woman from the settlement. But lately even that had been happening rarely . . . so rarely, in fact, that Odile sees more dying than are being born to repopulate their settlement.

Like her, the people are growing older, both the women who live underground and the men who survive on the outside—along with some women who prefer to live by themselves, away from settlements like Odile's.

The thought of women on the outside reminds her of Ash. Before Ash returned with what she thought was a book, Odile had known her only as one of the Vengers, nameless, seen around the tunnels and at Songtimes. But her courage in standing up to Odile at the council meeting was impressive. Ash was one of the younger women; perhaps it was time for her to mate with one of the men they brought in.

Though Odile has to admit the idea of Ash with one of the sick, filthy raggedmen they find is distressing. When she was young, Odile was taken and the result was a baby who died in childbirth; she never allowed herself to be taken again after that.

Yet as chief elder, Odile knows that their group, like the world at large, will simply fade away if it is not repopulated. And the human race will disappear, like other species have.

And would that be so bad, she asks herself. Isn't that what their ultimate fate is? What is worth holding onto in this way of life? Starving, scrounging for everything, under constant threat of violence and disease . . .

She hears a commotion coming from the hallway. She was told that a quartet of raggedmen had been seen in the area by the Vengers, so the council had ordered Vesters outside. Perhaps this was them, returning.

Odile finishes her drink and stands. She hopes this is the case; stores are getting low, the feeders told her.

A new group of men would be a very timely find.

13

At the bay, there are not as many raggedmen as Ash had feared. She wonders where they are going, stumbling along as though in a daze, like the stunned and blank-eyed survivors of a series of cascading catastrophes that they are.

They seem sick and frail; passing near them she hears wet coughs. They look like walking skeletons, their outer clothes hanging loose on their bones.

Still, there are enough raggedmen around to worry her. All it would take would be two of them and no matter how weak they are, she would be outnumbered. She is on high alert as she walks through the town toward the shore of the bay, watching for structures that resemble the one where she had met the man who first told her about the book.

But there are no buildings left. The wooden ones had been torn down for firewood back when there were still winters, and the brick ones have collapsed. She sees nothing like the school where she found the man with the book.

As the chief elder had instructed, she turns so that the big water stays on her right hand and continues her journey to the next school.

By the time she finds another structure that might be a possibility, she has not eaten for two full days. She is weak and dizzy, but presses on.

The building is the highest one standing, and it is relatively undamaged, on the outside, anyway. She stands before it, and notices designs carved in stone above the front door.

BAYSIDE COLLEGIATE SCHOOL

She has no way to figure out what the design means.

The building is still intact, so Ash knows it will likely be occupied by squatters. She walks around the town a few times to make sure she isn't being followed, then approaches the building again cautiously.

Once she sticks her head inside, she realizes that the outside of the building is deceptive. Inside it is as wrecked as the other buildings near her own settlement.

The ground floor will be the most dangerous, she knows. That's where there is the greatest chance of squatters. She walks inside, and, sure enough, in the dim interior sees raggedmen filling the corners and lining the walls of the large open ground floor chamber, reclining on their backs and sides.

The smell of them turns her stomach, not only the sour man-stench of stale sweat on never-washed bodies, but the reek of their body fluids, including the nauseating odor of pus and gangrenous limbs. These men are desperately sick. She hears their groaning. They have come into this sanctuary to drag up, she realizes, because they can no longer live outside.

They pose no immediate danger to her.

They watch her with dull, disinterested eyes as she steps past them, their heads swiveling, swaddled in whatever rags or old clothes they could find to protect themselves from the poisonous air outside. But swaddling is not the answer; the light itself is toxic, the atmosphere they breathe every day above ground is dangerous. That's why the women live underground and only come up for short periods. It isn't even safe to do that, but it is safer than wandering in the above world the way these raggedmen do.

She has heard there are some underground tribes of women where men are welcomed, but has never seen one. Most men have either been rejected by the tribes for being too violent, or else they are too crazy to consider joining an underground tribe.

Ash knows there were many women who fought in the wars, but they either joined underground tribes (many becoming Fisers, channeling their post-traumatic rage and psychoses for the benefit of their tribes through the sacrifices the tribe requires), or else find themselves one of the casualties of life in the Upground.

Not that living underground is any guarantee of survival. Everyone is dying; some are just dying more slowly than others.

Ash makes her way through the fug of disease to an open doorway at the side of the building that leads to stairs going up and down. The ones going up seem to be mostly intact, but the ones leading to a lower level are filled with rubble and impassable. If what she seeks is down there, it is lost forever.

She begins climbing the stairs. She doesn't know where the book would be hidden if it is here, but she is determined to find it if it exists.

She starts at the top floor, which was where she found what she thought was the book in the other building. It occurs to her that she might find something else that she thinks is a book, but which is not. She puts the thought out of her mind; the chief elder has told her what to look for this time, and given her a picture of what it looked like. She knows she will recognize it when she sees it.

Her search is slow. There are many small rooms here that she must look through. Unlike the other building, however, the roof has not fallen in, so the only light she has to work with is the light that filters through the dirt-caked windows on the outside walls. This means the inside rooms are in almost total darkness.

She picks through the rooms for hours. When she finishes with the top floor, she goes down to the next level.

The evening comes on, and the light that comes through the windows dims. But there is enough sun for her to continue working.

She knows she cannot leave the building to roam the streets at night, and she does not relish the thought of staying downstairs with the sick men on the first floor, so she keeps searching until exhaustion overtakes her.

Tired and hungry as she is, she lets herself slip into sleep in the detritus on the floor of the room she finds herself in on the third level.

14

She jerks awake to find a figure leaning against the wall, staring at her.

A man. She can smell it.

His face is wrapped in rags except for the eyes, but his head is uncovered and the skin on his bare scalp is filled with angry weeping blisters. From his posture he looks as sick as all the other men she has seen in the outside.

He wears a filthy coat that hangs from an emaciated frame. Ash is still groggy with sleep and hunger and doesn't have time to react when he removes a hand from under his garment. A panic seizes her—he is holding a rusty knife blade. His arm is shaking badly.

Where is her staff?

Beside her. She grabs it up and jumps to her feet.

As soon as her attacker realizes she will not be easy prey, he turns and stumbles out the door the way he came.

She hears him holler something. He must be part of a raiding party. She needs to leave.

She grabs up her pack and looks around frantically to see if she has left anything in her exhaustion of the night before.

Under a broken desk she spies an object—as long as the span of her hand from thumb to little finger and half as wide, and with the thickness of one of her fingers—that she recognizes from the chief elder's drawing.

She snatches it out of the debris on the floor and stashes it in her pack. She will examine it later, when she has more time.

Even now she hears an urgent clatter outside the room. The sound of feet running up a set of stairs. More than one, she thinks.

There is a second door at the other side of the room from the hallway. *Fast!* Ash orders herself.

Trembling now in fear, Ash pushes the door open and as she closes it behind her hears the sounds of men's voices coming from the room she has just left.

She enters a long hallway and as fast as she can manage she races down to the other end, where in the darkness of the corridor she sees stairs lit by the dim light from the outside.

She rushes down the stairs, pausing on the second landing to catch her breath. When she can move ahead without loud telltale panting, she creeps down the last flight of stairs to the ground floor.

What she sees chills her.

15

Back at the settlement in the abandoned nickel mine, Odile watches the four raggedmen being herded into the holding pen. They seem to be a sicker batch than usual—coughing, weak, emaciated. But still they are men, so they growl at the Vesters and rage at each other like subhumans. Perhaps it's fortunate that no male children have been born in the settlement recently, if they would turn into these creatures when they matured.

The men are getting worse, Odile thinks, both in their health and in the character of their behavior. And therefore so are we. She remembers Ash was almost taken on her last trip out, and sadness overwhelms her. Maybe we shouldn't continue, Odile thinks. Maybe it is right that this should be the end.

She turns away from the men before the Fisers come. She has still not seen Mae this morning, so she goes looking for her.

She stops by the Council chamber and is stunned to see the Council is in session.

They are in the middle of debating something loudly, but stop as soon as Odile enters the chamber.

"What is this?" she demands.

All eyes turn to Ells, who is sitting in Odile's accustomed spot at the center of the semi-circle of elders.

She is wearing Odile's laurel of dead branches.

"Eh?" Odile says. "What goes on?"

"Sit," Ells says.

"Leave my place."

"Your place nay longer."

"Who says this?"

"Council say. Chief elder no more."

"Oh? And why is that?"

Instead of replying, Ells says, "Where is Venger Ash?"

"First answer my question. Explain this."

"Ash is not in her rest chamber. Her work leader says she is not out scavenging. Where is she?"

"In the Upground."

"To do what?"

"To find the book."

"Who approved this?" Ells demands.

"*I* sent her. No other approval is necessary."

Ells resettles herself. She lets Odile's words sink in for the rest of the Council. Which, Odile now notices, does not include Mae.

"Council say she nay go. Odile agreed, then say she go," Ells says to the elders. "Odile defy Council. There is my right to remove you," she tells Odile.

"Right according to who?" Odile asks.

"Law of Council," Ells responds. She raises a hand, and three of the guards step forward. Ells flicks a wrist at Odile, and the guards move to surround her, boxing her in with their staffs.

"Pen," Ells says, and the trio begin to push Odile out of the chamber.

But she stops and resists them. They look to Ells for direction.

"Where is Mae?" Odile asks.

"Mae refused the will of Council."

"Where is she?" Odile repeats.

"Banished."

"What?!"

"Mae refused the will of the Council. I banished her to the Upground. It is the law of the Council."

"Banished when?"

"Today."

"Why wasn't I informed?"

No one answers her.

"What right," Odile begins, but before she can finish her sentence Ells points the top of her head to the chamber entrance, and the guards hold on to Odile. "No," she cries, "I have to look for Mae!"

But the guards push her the rest of the way out of the chamber. She struggles but they are too strong, and no longer recognize her authority as Council elder. They take her down to the holding pen where the men were kept. The men are gone, and the room is empty though their stench remains.

The guards push Odile toward one of the stone benches cut into the wall. Then two of them leave and the third stands outside the entrance to the room, her staff blocking the door so Odile cannot leave.

Odile collapses on the bench and puts her head in her hands and sobs in sadness and anger at what they have done to Mae.

Because of me, she thinks. Because of me.

16

Ash sees the men lying in the corners of the chamber sprawled with their throats cut or else their bodies pierced by knives. A half-dozen raggedmen stand above them stripping the clothes off the dead men and rifling through their belongings. The one who burst in on Ash on the upper level must have been part of this same group of bandits.

One of them notices Ash and grunts something to the others. They stop and stare at her. The bandit who first noticed her leaves the body he is stripping and leaps across the floor after her.

She sprints away as fast as she can go in her exhausted, starved condition, thinking, *No no, can't be caught, no.*

She makes it outside the building and clambers over the piles of rubble into a field that might have once been a farm but is now nothing but dead brush and dirt. There is no shelter out here, nothing to hide behind, so she keeps running.

Except the man who is chasing her is gaining on her. She throws a quick look behind and notices that another raggedman has joined the chase. They can't know I'm a woman, she thinks; I'm dressed as a man. They are doing this for whatever they can steal from me. Or just out of naked blood lust.

But once they find out she is a woman, she knows what will happen.

The raggedman from the building is almost up to her. Yet another raggedman appears to join the chase, so three are after her. Now she knows she has no chance to outrun them. She feels herself slowing down as her energy fades and the pains in her feet and legs overwhelm the fear.

Out of options, she will not make it easy for them. Let them come. She will not go without a fight.

She slows so the closest raggedman is almost up to her. She turns as she skids to a halt and thrusts the sharp point of her staff out to meet the closest running man.

Who, unable to stop or slow himself down, impales himself on the point of the staff. She hears a sharp CRACK as the staff pierces his chest.

His momentum knocks her over. She kicks him off of her staff and rolls to her feet.

When the other two raggedmen see what has happened, they slow. One peels off and runs away, but the other hesitates a moment, then comes straight at her. From under his coat, he withdraws a long, broad knife and comes at her with it, holding it over his head as though meaning to slice her in two down the middle.

Untrained in combat—she was a Venger, not a Vester—she is not sure how to fight this man one-on-one. She thrusts her staff toward him, but he lops off one end with a swing of the blade.

He keeps coming and she backpedals, terrified at the whooshing of the blade as he swings it closer and closer. He circles her and backs her into the body of the raggedman she has just killed. She trips over it and falls backward. She rolls out of the way as the blade comes down and misses her by inches.

It embeds in the body of the dead raggedman and gives her enough time to push the sharp end of her staff into her attacker as he struggles to free his blade.

The staff pierces his shoulder.

He cries out, but it is not a killing blow.

He works the blade free from the dead raggedman and winds up to cut her in two, but before that happens she swings the staff with all her might and strikes him on the side of his head.

The blow stuns him and sends him reeling backward and she steps forward and drives the point of her staff into his chest and that finishes him. Trembling, she pulls the staff out of his prone body and sends it into him again and again. She hears a furious screaming and is shocked to discover it is coming from her.

Her fury spent, she stands above the two bodies, panting and shivering.

In the distance, she notices a group of raggedmen gathering, watching this display. The group begins drifting toward her.

It was the scream, she realizes—a woman's yell, attracting them.

She pulls a water container from one of the dead men and then turns and runs as hard and fast as she can until she is away from any marauders.

She makes her way back to the river bed, where she finds a place to hide from the raggedmen drifting toward the bay. She stops at a low point in the ground where she won't be visible.

She sits for a while, catching her breath and scanning the area for trouble at the same time as she tries to calm herself. She is still trembling. It takes a while before she stops.

When her hands no longer shake, she removes the book from her sack. This is the thing responsible for all this . . . the journey, the killings. She has never seen anything like it. The front and back of it are hard, like clothes that are stiff with blood. And the inside has individual pieces attached together like softer versions of the front and back, flexible like Odile's wavering hands as she tried to explain what the book looks like.

Every page is covered with marks Ash can't understand, as well as some pictures. She has never seen a world as colorful as the one in this book. She turns the sheets, but, realizing it is useless because she can't figure out any of it, she returns it to her sack and sits back to wait for the night.

Was this the book the man Jo was looking for in the building she was originally scavenging? She has no way of knowing; she will have to return this to the chief elder and ask her what it is.

She waits until the sun is at its dimmest in the night, and starts back toward her settlement.

17

The trek back is inconsequential. She has no further episodes with raggedmen.

The guards at the entrance to her settlement at first prevent her from entering. They are hostile to her, in fact. They challenge her and bar the entrance with their staffs.

She remembers she is dressed as a man. In the shade of the overhang above the entrance to the mine, she unwraps the rags from her head to show her face.

"Ash," she says.

After much discussion, they finally allow her in, but they keep their distance from her. They don't know if she has become infected with the diseases that the men carry, the blister illness, the radiation sickness, whatever it is that turns them so rabid.

And she doesn't know, either; she may well be bringing illness into the tribe.

There is no one to greet her, no one to usher her to the Council chamber. No members of the Council anywhere.

Puzzled, she wanders through the tunnels back to her work chamber without seeing anyone. The living area for her unit is empty, too, when she gets back to that. Not unusual for this time of day, when most of the Vengers are out doing their work. Still, the eerie silence of the tunnels seems to have penetrated this space, too.

Something has changed, she thinks. The settlement feels different; though it is emptier, a tension charges the air that is new since she has been gone.

For now she is too hungry and tired to worry about it. All she wants to do is change out of her filthy, possibly infected clothing, and find something to eat. This is outside the regular eating hours, but she might be able to persuade the feeders to give her something.

As soon as she starts to strip the stinking rags from her body, two guards appear. Without a word, they each take an arm and pull her out of the chamber, even though she would be willing to go with them if they would only tell her what is happening.

They take her through the tunnels to the Council chamber. She is weak from hunger and thirst; she has not eaten for days. Why are they doing this before she can get sustenance? Didn't she do exactly what they asked her to do?

The Council is in session. All the elders are there, sitting around the semi-circle.

No, wait, two are missing, she sees. The chief elder and Mae are not there. Where are they? And why is Ells sitting in the chief elder's spot? She wears the chief elder's laurel wreath. Has something happened to the chief elder?

Fear grips her. The chief elder was her champion, she said she would protect Ash; what will happen to her now?

The guards leave Ash to stand in the same place she stood before, where all the elders can see her.

They let her stand, under their scrutiny, without saying a word. She wavers on her feet. She does not know if she can stand much longer before keeling over from hunger and thirst.

At last Ells says, "Ash."

Ash tries to focus on her voice, the blurry image of Ells's face. So tired. So hungry.

"Ash," Ells says again.

"Eat," Ash makes herself say. "Please."

"First talk. Then food."

Ash raises her hands in a gesture of protest. Her hunger and exhaustion have driven her past the deference she knows she must show to the Council.

"Council told Ash nay look for book," Ells says. "Why Ash go?"

Ash reaches into her sack where she has stashed her prize. "Find book," she says. She brings out the object she has brought back and holds it out to Ells. Ash shows it to the others, but no one tries to take it from her.

"Book," she says again.

"Council said nay book," Ells says. "Book evil. Book from *man*." She spits the word out. "Man evil, Council say."

Ash shakes her head. "Book important," she says. "Important."

Ells glares at Ash with burning eyes, as though she wants to rise and throttle the younger woman for her impudence in contradicting her.

"How you know?" Ells demands. "You read?"

"Nay. Man say. Man, Jo, say—"

"*Man say*," Ells says, and looks around at the other elders as though this proves her point. They nod in agreement with her. Man evil, therefore book evil.

"Why Ash get?" Ells asks. "Council say nay get."

"Chief elder," Ash says, "send Ash. Say get, bring back."

"Chief elder," Ells says, her mouth twisted, and again looks around.

"Chief elder say, book important," Ash adds. "Say give to her."

She holds up the book, offering it to them. Surely someone on the Council would be able to decipher the marks in the book and see the chief elder was right.

Again, no one makes any attempt to retrieve the book.

Ash summons all her courage and says, "Where chief elder? She tell."

"Ash want chief elder?" Ells says.

Ash nods.

Ells pats herself on her chest. "Chief elder now."

"No," Ash begins. Odile is the chief elder, she wants to say, but catches herself. The dark look on Ells's face stops her.

Ells holds up a hand and the two guards close in on Ash. "Ash want Odile?" Ells asks. "Take away."

This time Ash resists. "No!" she cries. "Eat! Please! No food! No food since—"

They pull her away.

18

They lead her to the area that is reserved for men who are brought back to the settlement. It is essentially a room dug into a distant area of the mine, away from the living areas in case the men bring with them infections from the upper world.

Now there are no men here, just their smell, vile, stomach-turning.

The space is dark, lit only by a single flickering torch. When her eyes grow accustomed to the darkness, Ash sees Odile, sitting cross-legged on a stone ledge.

A sentry is still standing at the entrance, preventing the two women from leaving.

When Odile sees Ash, she stands and rushes to embrace the younger woman. Ash takes a step back. She is confused; she has never been held by anyone, let alone this woman, who lately was the chief elder. In fact, this is the first time anyone has ever lain hands on her for anything other than a beating.

She doesn't know what to make of it.

Feeling Ash's discomfort, Odile releases her and holds her at arm's length. "You brought back the book?" she asks quietly.

Ash shows the elder the book, which she has been allowed to keep since no one else is interested in it.

Odile takes the book from Ash, and holds it, turns it around in her hands as though it were holy. Lovingly she rubs dirt off the outside of it.

"The book, nay?" Ash asks.

"Aye," Odile says, "the book."

She takes Ash by the hand and walks her back to the stone. She pulls Ash down to sit beside her.

"Ever seen a book before?" Odile asks.

"Once," Ash says. "Man who told me about this showed me. Book of 'po-tree,' he say."

"Did he read you any?"

Ash shakes her head. She recalls how she found him when she returned with what she thought was the book—dead, his clothes soaked with his blood, the book of poetry gone along with his pack, taken by the men who killed him.

"Too bad," Odile says. "Poetry is like the songs I sing. Only better. I remember poetry from my childhood. Books were banned many, many years before either of us was born. But some were still around after the Purge. People saved them as long as they could. They had to hide them. And gradually, even those disappeared. Along with books, we also lost the skill to understand them."

Again, so many words. Ash concentrates, but she doesn't grasp everything Odile is saying.

"Nay see book since?" Ash asks.

Odile shakes her head. "Not since I was a girl," she says.

It seems strange, Ash thinks, hearing the chief elder talk about herself as a girl. Ash cannot imagine this woman ever being young.

Or the world ever being different.

"Even before books were gone," Odile says, "wisdom was handed down through Singers. No one was allowed to read, you see. So the only way we could keep knowledge alive was by singing songs about it. My mother was a Singer, like her mother, and her mother. They taught me the old wisdom from the Before, and the story of the tribe. Once, books transmitted this. Wisdom, and learning. Without books, Singers pass on our history."

"What is 'history'?" Ash asks.

"The story of the group. In the Before, all could have book wisdom. Most could read. But when war came, and riots over food and water, books were the last thing on people's minds. Some of us were taught to read as children, and we learned to appreciate the wisdom in books."

Ash waits for the chief elder to say more.

"Ells was right," Odile goes on, "books nay protect us, nay feed us. But when you said the man told you about the book, I knew we had to see it, even if the Council said nay. There might be something here we can use, some wisdom to ease our lives. Some way to save ourselves from this." She looks around the chamber.

Ash listens to all those words, and tries to make the translation for herself: the book may save us.

"And you," Odile says, "you brought this back. By yourself."

Ash nods.

Odile draws Ash into her arms again for a hug. At first Ash resists, but the elder holds Ash until Ash stops squirming and allows herself to be enfolded by Odile's warm arms. It is a feeling she has never had before. She could not even begin to describe it, it is so foreign to her experience. But she gives herself up to it.

Feeling Ash relax into her embrace, knowing it is probably the first kindness Ash has ever been shown, moves Odile more than even Ash. Odile wipes tears from her eyes.

Ash taps her on the arm, raises her hands, and looks around.

"Why here?" Ash asks.

The older woman sighs. "Most things change. But human nature doesn't. Old ways drag up hard. I'm sorry they brought you here with me."

"Where is Mae?" Ash asks.

The elder takes a moment before she answers. "Gone."

"Gone?"

"Sent away. The Upground," Odile murmurs. "She resisted Ells. Then she was put out. To drag up."

"Maybe not," Ash says. She has seen women on the outside. Not many, it's true, but she knows it's possible for them to survive by themselves.

"Maybe not," Odile agrees, but Ash can tell she doesn't believe it. Odile gives her a weak, sad smile and reaches out to cup Ash's cheek.

Odile returns her attention to the book. She holds it in her hands, admiring it. She opens it, looks at the sheets inside, turning them over, one by one, slowly, with reverence. "Do you know what this says?" she asks Ash.

Ash shakes her head.

"I will read. But later." Odile sets it beside her. "First you need to eat."

At last, something Ash understands. Eat.

Ash nods.

"You must be starving. Wait there."

She retrieves a bundle wrapped in a corner of the room. The bundle is filled with strips and chunks of cooked and dried meat. The chief elder offers it to Ash, who attacks the food with both hands. It tastes slightly off, as though it were old, but Ash doesn't care. She is ravenous.

After she eats her fill, Odile says, "Now sleep. We'll talk more after."

Ash doesn't need to be told twice. She stretches out on the stone ledge and, regardless of her discomfort, her hunger is sated and she falls asleep at once.

19

Odile sits with the book in her lap and begins to read. She was taught to read so long ago that she is unused to decoding words. So it is slow work by the light of the torch that is the holding pen's only illumination.

She reads:

REPORT OF THE UNITED NATIONS COMMISSION ON THE GLOBAL ENVIRONMENTAL CRISIS

2155

Edited by
Joost Keijzer, Ph.D.
Co-Chair
UN Commission
University of Amsterdam

Jacynthe Renate, Ph.D., M.P.H.
Co-Chair
UN Commission
University of Toronto

Chapter 1: Executive Summary
Chapter 2: Introduction and Context
Chapter 3: Drivers of Global Catastrophe
Chapter 4: Data and Current State of Knowledge
Chapter 5: Air
Chapter 6: Biodiversity
Chapter 7: Oceans and Water
Chapter 8: Land and Soil

```
Chapter 9: Conclusions: Too Late?


Chapter 1: Executive Summary


In 2155, the remaining countries comprising the
United Nations convened a Commission on the
Global Environmental Crisis with the goal of
producing a report on the current state of the
cascading  global  environmental,  social,  and
political cataclysms, and the bleak outlook for
the future.


Despite decades of warnings, the negative effects
of environmental climate change have multiplied
irreversibly, and the continued effects on global
social organizations will be catastrophic.


Consider the following examples.
```

There follow pages of words, numbers, charts, and tables. She recognizes words that are repeated throughout: *instability, unsustainability, thawing, rising, failure, ecosystem collapse, biodiversity destruction, methane explosions, mass extinctions, radiation exposure.* She knows some of these words because they are part of the lore that has been passed down the generations, the lore she shares in her songs.

Or *shared*, perhaps. Because will she still sing the tribe's songs, now that she is no longer the chief elder, or even a Council member? Can she sing them, in her imprisonment?

And does she still *want* to?

What good will it do now? What good will this book do? What good would it do to know how they have gotten to this point? The question now is, what could be done? What could they accomplish knowing what is in this book—a small group of slowly dying survivors, squabbling among themselves for the illusion of power even at the end?

And yet, she thinks, if there is any chance this book can help them, she must continue.

It takes her many days, reading slowly by the poor light where they are kept prisoner, but she finishes through to the last chapter, headed, "Conclusions: Too Late?" She reads through one of the sections of the chapter, "Population Displacement." She sees maps like the one she had given Ash, and reads this sentence:

> Among the many migrations brought on by social, political, agricultural, and ecological disasters across the globe, northern Canada and Siberia may become migratory destinations. The outlook for food production, however, is still grim due to the anticipated heat and inhospitable soil conditions worldwide. If agriculture is possible anywhere, it will likely be in these locations.

Migratory destinations. She puzzles through the words. So near to comprehension, and so far.

Ash returned from her journey without the pack that Odile had given her, so the folding map she had is gone. But she remembers that they are already in what was once northern Canada. She rifles through the book and finds a map that looks like the one Ash had. She finds where they are now, and sees that there are areas further north, all the way up as far as the land mass goes, before the vast sea where melted polar ice used to be.

Would it be worth moving the tribe north? Going out into the dangers of the Upground?

Not without scouting it first, she realizes, to make sure this is actually someplace to go that would be better than where they are now.

Still, Odile thinks, such an exploration might save them. She has been part of this settlement since her birth, and she knows conditions have never been as bad as they are now. If they don't try something, they will become the next group to succumb to extinction.

How much smarter the people must have been at that time, she thinks, to be able to write reports like this. And yet, it seems like they did nothing with their knowledge. So their wisdom was worthless.

This learning has gone out of the world, she considers. It will never be recovered. So what do we have now?

She gazes down at Ash, sound asleep on the stone ledge. The young woman's legs twitch. Perhaps she is dreaming of being chased, Odile thinks.

Ash has almost recovered from her ordeals, Odile reflects. She knows that Ash had been attacked by a group of men on her first journey, and returned starving and near-delirious from the second journey, when she returned with the book. Who knew what other horrors she has seen in these trips outside?

Has she, Odile, doomed Ash with her latest quest to find a book that may not be as useful as she had hoped? There were some dangers that she knew Ash had been exposed to—the marauding gangs of men in the outside, for example—but there were other dangers, other illnesses, especially, that Ash could have brought back with her. Some infectious, some not; the infectious ones had the possibility of wiping out the entire settlement. The non-infectious ones, like sickness from exposure to the sunshine, would carry off Ash alone.

Still, there aren't many who would have been as brave as Ash. Since she returned, Odile has been trying to teach Ash to read from the book, and Ash has been picking up the learning quickly.

Odile has even been telling Ash some of the lore contained in the songs that Odile knows. She was training Mae to step into the role of Singer after Odile would be gone, but now Ells has ensured that will never happen.

Someone else must learn to become the Singer. Ells has no interest in it, but the wisdom of the tribe must be handed down, and only Odile has that knowledge. Odile has not told Ash of her plan to train her as a Singer, but it is something they will have to discuss soon.

The thought of Mae brings a new wave of sadness over her.

She is sitting like that, head in her arms folded across her knees, crying for what the tribe has lost—and what she personally has lost in her companion Mae's death—when a contingent from the Council of elders approaches the area where she and Ash are being held.

20

Five elders stand silently beside the guard at the entrance. At a nod from one of the women, the guard steps aside and they enter.

Ells is not among the group.

"Odile," one of them says.

Odile rises to meet them. She stands and waits for them to explain their business, these elders who have betrayed her.

The elder who spoke looks at Ash, still asleep, and then at the book on the ground. "You read?" the elder says, indicating the book.

Instead of answering, Odile says, "Why are you here?"

The elders share guilty looks, then another one of them says, "Apologize."

Odile stretches to her full height. "Never."

The others look at each other again. One of them says, "Nay. We come to apologize to you."

Odile says nothing.

"We have talked," the elder says. "Ells was wrong. If you say the book is important, then the book is important."

"Where is Ells?" Odile asks. "Where are the others? Why don't they come?"

They have no answer.

Instead, the leader of the contingent says, "Have you read it?"

Odile nods.

"Tell us," the elder asks, "it is important?"

Odile looks from one to the other of the five women. "*Now* you want to know about the book?"

They all say aye.

"You keep us in the Fisers pen," Odile says, "with no way to get out. You make Ells the chief elder. Now you want me to tell you about the book?"

When no one answers, Odile says, "Nay. Go."

No one moves, and this time she shouts, "*Go!*"

Her shout wakes Ash, who sits up and looks around in total confusion, then gapes when she sees the Council members standing around Odile.

"Please," one of the elders says.

"For the sake of the tribe," says another.

"What is the tribe doing for me?" Odile asks. She holds up her hands, offering the vile chamber as an example of how they have treated her.

"Ells keeps you here," one of the elders says. "We tried reasoning with her to let you out, but she says nay."

"Then I say nay."

"But you are the Singer," another of the elders implores. "You are our history-keeper."

Odile shakes her head. "The chief elder is always the Singer. Go ask Ells. Tell her to read the book and sing of it."

"Please," the first elder says. "Ells is not interested. Ells knows *nothing*. We need you. The people need you."

The rest of the elders nod in agreement.

"You should have thought about that before you put me here. Now go."

"Please," they all say now.

Odile considers that, and shares a glance with Ash. Then she says, "I will sing the book. But not to you alone. To all the people."

The elders agree at once.

The speaker for the group says, "You will sing tonight?"

"Nay. Tomorrow. After first feed. Get the people together, I will sing the book then."

The elders nod gratefully. It is settled. They are visibly relieved.

They file out and Odile turns to Ash. "You heard?" Odile asks.

Ash nods. "You are going to sing the book?"

Under Odile's tutelage, she has been practicing her language skills, as well as her reading skills.

"Aye," Odile says. "At first I said nay, not until they released us from here. But then I had an idea, and said aye."

"Good," Ash says.

She begins to cry.

"Oh," Odile says. "What's the matter?"

"Maybe this will save the tribe?"

Odile lets the question hang.

We'll see tomorrow, she thinks.

21

The next morning, after the first feed, the elders collect as much of the tribe together as can be spared. It is a small group, less than fifty, including most of the work groups and the small number of old men who survive. Some members cannot be spared from their duties—the Vesters and the Fisers have to keep working or else the tribe will starve, so only a handful of them are in the main chamber.

Also present are Ells and the three elders who are loyal to her, including one whom Ells has appointed to take Mae's place. They stand at the rear of the group. Ells has rightly guessed that this is Odile's attempt to re-establish her place as the head of the Council of Elders, and Ells is determined to not let that happen. If the other members of the Council wish it, she will have to persuade them as she did before that Odile is not worthy of leading them.

Odile herself appears at the front of the room, and the members of the tribe pound the floor of the chamber with their palms as a form of welcome. Ash follows her, holding the book before her like a sacred vessel.

Odile seats herself on the ground at the front of the chamber and waits. Those assembled know this is the time to get settled and prepare to listen to their Singer, the knowledge-keeper who sings them stories of their past. If the tribe has anything sacred in these dark times, it is songs from the Singer.

Odile waits. Then she reaches out toward Ash, who hands her the book. She holds it up, then lowers it to the ground in front of her.

She closes her eyes.

22

When Odile had sung in the past, Mae had beaten a steady rhythm on the ground with her hands. Odile keenly feels Mae's absence, and a wave of sadness overwhelms her.

She waits, steadies herself, and begins her song.

> *"Listen! Lend me, sisters,   leave to sing my song,*
> *Tribe-chest of the tales   that teach our Before.*
> *This ancient book, banished,   forbidden*
> *By the Council of Elders, cowards,   caring not*
> *What wise words   dwell within,*
> *Thinking it tainted   by the tongue of man*
> *Which Ash alone   agreed to find*
> *Daring the destruction   of our dirty world*
> *To bring back   this book of wisdom*
> *So learn we might how life   was lived in the Before*
> *And how we might make   more for the tribe*
> *As the Ahead-times   emerge from the mornings."*

Odile pauses while the tribe processes her words, which are understandable but strange to them, the remnants of an archaic language that is all the more magical for being so foreign-sounding. But the hypnotic chant keeps them rooted to where they sit.

She continues.

> *"Once, there was   a wicked war.*
> *The sear of a thousand suns   struck the earth*
> *And burnt the ground bare   so the beasts disappeared*
> *And destroyed the flowers and food   and all fair life*
> *And split the earth into   the bright and the darkness*

And drove us down   deep into the ground
To wallow like worms   in wretched darkness.
But even before the bombs   and the blood, the earth,
Ravaged, took her revenge   for the ruthless ways
The people of the past   poisoned her,
Overwhelmed the oceans   with such evil
That all the creatures could not   continue
To live, so they left us   forlorn and forgotten
Winged or walking   warm-blooded or cold
With furry feet, fins,   or feathers
And the earth dragged up first   ahead of the bombs.
But the men it drove mad,   monsters they became
Whose bloodlust, kindled by battle   and brewed in the stew
Of life lived above—   the long drought,
The blister bane   that blights all it touches—
Encouraged us as enemies   eternal, until
Found by Vesters, they fill   their function to nourish us
And siring the sons and daughters   who save our numbers.
So underground our tribe lives   uncertain and afraid.
This ancient book   I offer before you
Which the council conceived   as keeping evil
Under the authority   of usurper Ells
Tells us the truth   and I will tarry not
To explain our alternatives   for avoiding our end
If we wish to walk   our way for longer."

She pauses again, to allow the tribe to catch up to her meanings and to gather her strength.

Then she lifts the book above her head and goes on.

153

"Our food is failing,   failing too the tribe.
The ground no longer gives   good stock,
The water upon which   we rely, our lifeblood,
Poisons all people   who perhaps must drink it
And even the only food   we ever eat
The stock that sustains us   arrives sick
More and more,   that meagre sustenance
Whose numbers disappear daily   no matter the devices
We use to entice them   underground.
The ancient book I bear   above me
I studied for certain weeks   and sure am I
That wisdom's words   it whispers to us
From the time before the bombs   and blood,
A hope it holds,   hazy though it may be,
Difficult, dangerous,   with doubtful success.
If we are to win   our wars with death
We can no longer linger   our lives at this place.
We must move   from our mine's safety."

As Odile knew it would, this causes an unsettling throughout the chamber. She sets the book down and waits for silence. When the chamber is again quiet, she continues.

"The wisdom-chest, collecting   clues from the Before
Proposes a province   north of the place
Where we now stay, safe   aye, yet slowly dragging.
The horrible heat   that hurts us so
Is less, and likewise   at least some chance exists
That food we may find there,   and fertile ground,
The familiar food   of the fruitful earth.

People passing there   peaceful may be.
There may we thrive   and there may we live.
So says the book,   this simple message
Waiting only upon   one of us
Who, determined and daring,   will leave our dim mine
Where drag-up awaits us   one and all
And detect this destination,   discover this place
And return to tell us   where the tribe must go.
To tell the book's brave sense   you begged me,
And thus truly have I sung   to the tribe this day."

With that, Odile falls silent.

23

Silence also falls across the chamber as the sound of Odile's voice dies away. Before long, one of the council elders stands. Like the rest of them, she is old and frail.

"The journey you sing of," she says, "I will make."

"Sister," Odile says, "thank you. I know you would. But the search will be hard. It must fall to a younger."

The elder stands for a moment longer, then, disappointed, sits. Odile looks out across her people. It seems they are all old, even the younger ones . . . their lives have left them fragile, pale from a lifetime spent out of reach of the sun's radiation, emaciated and covered with sores from too little of an unchanging and unhealthy diet.

No one else stands, no one raises a hand.

The members stare back at her. Their faces tell Odile all she needs to know; they look at her dully, uncertain and afraid. The problem is not a matter of failure of nerve, Odile knows, but failure of hope. They have lived so long without hope that no one even recognizes the possibility of it anymore.

Without another word, Odile hands the book back to Ash, then struggles to her feet. On painful legs, defeated, she limps out of the tribal chamber.

At the doorway, she pauses and turns. "I call a meeting of the Council of the Elders," she announces.

For the first time, Ells steps forward from where she has been standing in the rear of the chamber. "Nay, you may not," she says. "You are not a member of the Council. As chief elder, only I call meeting. Now I say to you elders: reject the plan Odile has given. It is dangerous. Our current location keeps us as safe as we will ever be. This plan is *foolish*."

She hits the last word hard, reminding them of how Odile called the Council foolish for not wanting the book.

"Moving from our home would be *foolish*, Ells continues. "It will only lead to grief. The book *lies*."

When none of the other council elders speak up for her, including the contingent of five who begged for this song, Odile inclines her head slightly in acceptance and leaves the chamber.

Ells watches her go, preening in triumph.

Odile returns to the holding area where she and Ash have been relegated.

Her plan failed.

Still carrying the book, Ash follows.

24

"What is there to do?" Ash asks.

"Not much now," Odile says. "No one will come forward. Ells controls the Council, and without the Council's approval nothing will happen. The ones Ells doesn't control have no reason to believe this will make any difference in their lives."

Ash shakes her head. "No," she says. "What is there to do on the journey?"

"The journey? Why? Are you thinking of going?"

Ash nods.

"Oh, Ash," Odile says. "This is no trip for you. It was enough you found the book and brought it back. You were hurt badly. The tribe owes you just for doing that."

"My head is better," Ash says.

Odile pats her shoulder with affection. "Besides, we are prisoners here. Who knows how long we have to stay? They would never let you go for fear you'd disappear and never come back."

"I would come back, Ash says stubbornly.

"*I* know you would," Odile says. "But the others don't. They would never let you go. All right? Settled?"

Ash mulls that over, says, "Aye."

After a while, she asks, "But what does the book say to do?"

Odile takes the book and opens it to a page with a map on it. She puts a gnarled finger on a spot on the map. "Here is our settlement." She moves her finger. "Here is where you found the book. The bay is much bigger now, so the shoreline you see here isn't accurate. But."

She traces a path around the bay toward the top. "This is where the book says there might be some hope. *Might be*," she emphasizes. "It's possible communities around here are growing food. This might be where the last agricultural outposts on earth are. But Ash, it's not certain."

Ash nods her understanding.

Odile waits all the rest of the day, but no one from the Council comes to her. She had thought the contingent from the day before might be the beginning of a revolt, but no . . . Ells must have persuaded them of the foolishness of her suggestion, and the rest, out of shame and fear, did not come.

This was our last chance, Odile thinks. If we don't take this, there truly is no hope for us. We are doomed and this long-abandoned mine will become our grave.

Ash is stretched out on the floor, asleep, when Odile arranges herself on the hard stone ledge of their chamber. The sentry stationed by the entrance to make sure they stay put watches her, then turns away.

Odile falls asleep, despairing that the dwindling group's last chance has faded.

When she wakes in the morning, Ash is gone.

PART III

The Third Journey

25

By the time the guard at the entrance to their cell wakes up and realizes what has happened, Ash is far away.

The people of the settlement are free to come and go, so the guards at the mouth of their mine paid her no attention when she appeared, wrapped head-to-toe in rags, and slipped away into the midnight sun.

She totes her pack with the map Odile had shown her in the book, which she carefully and quietly tore out of the book before she left. She also hauls as much water as her pack can hold; at night, most of the torches that illuminate the mine are extinguished, so she crept down the tunnels by touch to where the water was stored in ancient jugs and filled her carrier from that.

She also took as much food as she could find in their cell; she was certain Odile would understand. She is hopeful she will be able to find more food on her journey.

Hopeful. Not a word Ash would have used, she thinks, prior to her enforced imprisonment with Odile. But in all the time she spent with the chief elder (and Ash cannot think of the old woman in any other way), Odile has changed how she looks at their situation—not as a series of events that could never change, but as a circumstance that they might be able to influence, if they only knew how.

There might be some hope, Odile had said the night before.

And there was only one way to know for sure.

So Ash walks.

Many klicks up the road, she comes across what looks like a bundle of rags. As she draws near, she recognizes it as a body, and when she bends down to examine it, she unwraps the head and discovers the gentle features of Odile's friend, Mae.

Her eyes are cloudy and stare unseeing into the harsh and distant sky.

She does not appear to have been taken. Her clothes seem undisturbed, which means Ash is the first to find her. There is no water container nor any evidence of a food packet. So Ells sent her out with nothing. She was certain to drag up without anything to sustain her.

Using her staff, Ash digs a trough in the ocher dust large enough for Mae's slender body. She covers it over as best she can so Mae will not be found and abused by raggedmen.

There are no longer any prayers to say, and nothing to pray to, but Ash sits beside Mae's makeshift grave for a while, trying to comfort Mae's spirit, if it continues to linger. She wonders how she will tell Odile about this.

She says goodbye to the elder. Then she continues on her way.

Odile was right; the trip is long and difficult.

It takes three days to get to the town where she found the book, then she turns north and follows the bay. The hardest part is staying away from the raggedmen who also tramp north. Do they know where to go? She wondered if they had found their own book, or if it is just something men know. Or if they have a source of information that the women do not have.

Or, more likely, they just follow the men they see walking ahead of them, with no more idea of where they are going than she has.

She has no interest in getting close enough to any of them to ask.

The first part of her trip takes her through what used to be called the Canadian Shield, an arc of solid rock formations that are ages old. All the trees of the voluminous forest are dead, skeletal shapes good only for shade at certain times of the day, and to hide behind when men get too near.

It is rugged terrain. The rocks tear through the rags she wears around her feet. Here and there she finds men who have collapsed from exertion or sickness or starvation. She takes rags from their body to wrap around her feet, which are growing bloody and blistered from her walk.

She is not able to go as fast as she could when she started out. She covers less ground. She grows more tired by the day.

She makes her water rations last by mixing them with water from the bay that she follows. The water is drinkable, but she has no illusions that it is safe. She takes her chances. She just needs to survive long enough to find Odile's communities and return to the settlement with the knowledge of where they are.

She walks for two more days after her supply of food runs out. She is shaky and light-headed, but forces herself to continue, with more frequent stops.

When her strength has almost deserted her, she comes across two bodies, both men, a short distance apart. She kneels down beside each one and pokes him with her staff. They are dragged up for sure. There are signs of violence, blood on the men, disturbances in the dirt on the ground indicating a scuffle. Maybe they argued, she thinks, and killed each other.

She leans closer to sniff them. Relatively recent.

When she was younger and the elders were trying to find the best work unit for her based on her talents, they placed her on a stint with the Feeders. So she has some training in preparing bodies, including determining whether or not they are still good.

Both appear to have dragged up around the same time, so she chooses the one who looks slightly larger.

She finds a long, slender piece of rock in a nearby dry river bed, and hones it as best she can on the granite that makes up the landscape. When she is satisfied the rock is as sharp as she can get it, she uses it on the body.

She slices the muscles of the thighs and back into the familiar strips of meat that make up the diet of her tribe. It is not easy work with the sharpened rock—the Feeders have tools made especially for this job from scavenged metal—but she does it well enough. Too hungry to let the meat dry properly, and with no way to cook it to remove the sickness, she slakes her raging hunger at once, and saves some pieces wrapped in a rag to dry later.

This discovery strengthens her, and cheers her. There may be a source of food along this journey after all.

As with the water, she has no illusions that this meat is disease-free, but increasingly it doesn't matter; the hunger that racks her body makes such discretion beside the point. Anyway, niceties such as long-term thinking have mostly vanished for all but the rare elder, like Odile.

She continues north.

From every vantage point along her trek, she sees no signs of agricultural activity as Odile described from the pictures in the book. Whichever direction she looks, there are no patches of greenery. Nothing that looks like a community of people banded together. Ash wonders if they lived underground, as she did? And did they grow food underground, too?

If that's true, she may never find evidence of them, even though she looks for signs of underground dwellings. She searches every change in the landscape, every low point and every shadow in crags. She does not discover any tunnels or openings.

The weather does not change even slightly, either. The heat does not lessen, especially around the middle of the day. It is as burning hot as the sun outside her settlement. The heat penetrates the clothes that protect her head and her body and soak them with heavy sweat.

Following the waters of the bay, Ash continues on for two more weeks. The further she walks, the more blisters she gets on her feet, the shorter each day's distance is compared to the day before.

At a certain point, she decides to turn inland. She is still not entirely certain what she should be looking for, but nothing she has come across has given her any reason to believe the tribe should relocate here. She doesn't know, of course; it is not a decision that should be left to her, anyway. It is a decision for the elders to make. Her job is to search for some reason to move, and then make it back to the settlement to report what she finds.

She walks on. The further she gets from the bay, the fewer raggedmen she sees. What she can salvage from the remnants of others' killings have been what's sustained her thus far, but as she travels into the dry pampas inland, she finds fewer bodies, and her food begins to run out again. The raggedmen must know enough not to wander too far from the water.

In another week of walking inland, she gets to the bottom of her last water container. She is surrounded by what seem to be a thousand lake beds, but they are all dry. As she travels further from the bay, the water disappears entirely.

Still she continues on.

The shakiness that has plagued her grows worse. She takes more breaks to rest, and finds it harder to stand afterwards without dizziness making the world spin. She moves along by leaning on her staff; progress is slower than ever.

Finally she reaches a crest that allows her to survey the countryside for many klicks around. Nothing that looks like agricultural communities—nor any communities at all—as far as she can see in the blinding light of midday. The book must not have been true.

Either that, or the communities that once were here did not survive.

Regretfully, she decides there is no reason to continue in the direction she is going. Her mission changes in this instant from discovering a possible source of relocation for the tribe to getting back to her settlement with the news that there is no place to go.

Ells was right. The book lied.

She turns to make her way back.

And then she sees it.

26

It's in the distance, hazy and shimmering, but definitely there. Fields of green and gold, evenly spaced on the spit of land where the bay turns in, and, across an expanse of water, another stretch of green, geometric rows and squares so different from the endless dead plains of brown she has been walking through.

And she sees what look to be above-ground dwellings in a series of small villages, small wooden huts arranged in concentric circles.

It is all too far away for her to make out any people, but this must be what the book talked about, what she has come so far to find.

She takes in the sight for a few more minutes, trying to calculate how long it would take her to get to the villages she sees in the distance. Before going back, should she visit them first to make sure what she is seeing is real, and not a fever dream brought on by sickness?

Or should she go straight back toward her settlement and report what she has seen?

Nay, she decides, she has come this far, and she is so close (another handful or two of days' travel) that she has to go on and see these communities for herself. Perhaps she can rest, take some nourishment, and maybe bring one of these villagers back with her as proof of her find, if any will consent to come.

Rejuvenated by her discovery, Ash turns from the top of the crest and loses her footing.

She tumbles all the way down to the bottom of the rise.

When she reaches the bottom, hardpan like stone from years without rain, she hears a CRACK and feels a terrible pain in her leg. She tries to get up, but the pain shoots through her and she faints.

When she finally comes around, she opens her eyes into the furnace of the sun and immediately shuts them again and turns her head into the hardpan.

She doesn't know how long she has been lying there. In her fall, the rags around her head have come unraveled and trail behind her. She tries to pull them back but can't reach them, and when she tries to stretch out her arms, she moves the bottom part of her body and the pain shoots up to her hip.

Ash looks down and sees her foot splayed at an odd angle. She has no water left in her containers, and her food supply is gone. She can't walk—can't even move without excruciating pain.

The sun beats down without mercy.

She has found what Odile had sung about. There is vegetation, the signs of another colony. Hope for their tribe to relocate and possibly survive. But only if she can make it back to her settlement. How can she, now?

She has let Odile down. This, more than the pain in her leg, makes her squeeze out what meagre tears her dehydrated body can form.

27

Odile is once again seated in the chief elder's spot in the council chamber, at the head of the semi-circle of elders. Ells sits glaring at her from the end of the semi-circle.

The tribe is gathered in the chamber after the evening feeding to hear Odile's latest song. It has been over a month since she last saw Ash. When Odile realized Ash had gone, she assumed Ash had disobeyed her and left to discover the truth of the book.

In the weeks since Ash's disappearance, Odile has reclaimed her role as chief elder. As word of Ash's departure spread—and as more of the group came to believe that she left to find the land predicted by the book in Odile's song—those elders who supported Ells had one by one left her side and returned their support to Odile. Odile knows that what caused them to return to her was the hope that had spread among the members of the group—a hope that started with her last song about the book, and the possibility that there might be a different way of living than their current life underground.

They came to believe again in a concept of the future.

Odile sees it in the eyes of the other members of the council, as well as the workers whom she encounters in the tunnels. They look to her for courage as they never had before . . . as though the wisdom of the book had infused her and she became the vehicle for the tribe's salvation.

As they look to her now.

But what can she say?

Odile has no idea how far Ash went, or, indeed, whether or not Ash actually left to find what Odile has sung about. She only knows that the guard on duty at the entrance told her that Ash slipped away one night; she might have escaped to another destination altogether.

She might never come back.

Nay, Odile cannot believe that. Ash must have gone to find the northern settlements that the book suggested.

And if they were there, Ash will have found them.

Wouldn't she?

Now the tribe wants to hear from Odile. Wants another message of hope as the one she delivered before starts to fade in the uncertainty over Ash's journey.

Odile has tried sending out a silent message to Ash, where ever she is, and asking for guidance.

Receiving none, she sits before the tribe now, and prepares to sing.

She begins.

> *"Listen! Lend me, sisters,   leave to sing my song,*
> *Tribe-chest of the tales   that teach our Before.*
> *This story of the sorrows   that struck our elders*
> *A tale of wars and woes   and wasting illness*
> *That brought us, bereft,   to this heartbroken life*
> *Until one who finally faced   the frightened people*
> *And to them said, 'Savior   am I, sunlight*
> *In all the angry darkness that wars   against us.*
> *When the time was near   to weigh the future*
> *Of the tribe's time   and temporary fortune*
> *Ash it was who alone   of all the timid tribe*
> *Struck off, sincere   in her soul's quest*
> *To find the fertile soil   that may finally pledge*
> *The continued creation of life   for us, the concealed people.*
> *Nay thoughts of tribulations, trials   or troubles*
> *Held her, the hero,   from her hard choice*
> *To try and travel   though tired and hurt*
> *To find a far home   for her fortunate people."*

Odile pauses. She looks out over the faces of the women and the few old men who live in the settlement, assembled in the chamber to hear her.

There is a glint of something in their eyes that she has never seen before.

She knows how she must continue.

"Oh Ash, our gratitude abides   for all you have done
To save the secret people   in our sad world
Dim and dying   in our deep home.
On your return we rely   and remain in hope
That you, young traveler,   using your wits
Will bring back proof   of the book's truth
In what wise haste   we allow you to decide.
With such certainty we wait   for your wandering to end
And you return to renew us,   so, reborn,
Your tribe may travel   to where you tell us.
Thus truly have I sung   to the tribe this day."

She bows her head and signals the end of her song.

As is the custom, her listeners sit quietly, processing what she has told them. Even in the silence, Odile feels the new spirit in the chamber, a sense of possibility instead of the usual grim resignation. It is almost audible, a buzz as of the renewed blood pounding in the veins of the settlement

She gathers herself and returns to the chamber of the chief elder, which she again occupies. She is by herself. She lies on her pallet on the floor, wondering if she has done the right thing, rekindling her people's hope.

So much depends on Ash's return, which is not only far from certain, but, by now, highly doubtful.

Odile closes her eyes, and waits for sleep that does not come.

28

The next morning, two raggedmen find her.

They see Ash lying where she had fallen, but approach her carefully, one from each side, as hunters do.

When she rises up with a roar and flourishes her staff at them, they rush away.

Ash stands and watches them go, balanced on her one good leg. The other is braced by a splint she made from nearby timber wrapped around her leg with strips of material torn from her cloak.

She looks at the green and golden lands that lie off in the distance, and realizes in her current state she will never make it there. It is further away than she thought. Her only chance is to try returning to her home so she can let Odile know what she found. After she recovers from this trip, she can lead a large group back to this place, and then on to the green fields. A group well-prepared for the trek, as she has not been.

She memorizes the landscape so she can find this spot again. She will also have to take note of how many days it takes to get up here so she can report that to the tribe, too.

Sweating already from the heat, trembling from the terrible pain in her leg, and weak from lack of food, she starts on the long journey back to her settlement.

SILO SIX

BY
WENDY SURA THOMSON

CHAPTER ONE

Bailey woke up when the lights came on. The lights were harsh, indicating no dust storm above ground. Directly powered by the sun without the benefit of storage batteries, the lights reflected the daytime weather that no one ever saw. Bailey quietly rolled out of her sleep pod and headed to the communal washroom. She left a sleeping Ephraim – Ephraim, who could sleep through anything. When she returned, Ephraim was up and dressed, except for his shoes.

"Good morning, husband of mine." Bailey grinned and gave Ephraim a kiss on the cheek. "Hungry? We have extra credits left from last week. We can have a nice breakfast, if you want."

"Let's not squander them, Bales. You never know when we might need them." Ephraim finished slipping on his shoes and stood up. "I'll be right back." Ephraim headed to the washroom.

Bailey flipped on the information screen and watched the ticker-tape data scrolling across the screen.

Food rations: 465 days……. Shelter headcount…….. 2,865……….. Change from yesterday………. (25)…………. Interior air quality………….. 95%……………. Next scheduled receipt of supplies…………… 182 days…………………….Medicine stock status…………………… 90 days ……………………. Radiation index…………… high…………………….. Sunspot activity…………………… normal…………. Night travel advisory……. Significant windstorm possible for next 36 hours…….. Food rations: 465 days……..

The screen flickered, then went black for several seconds before sputtering back on, now filled with static. Bailey turned off the screen. The interference was happening more and more frequently. She took out the book she had checked out of the library and perched on the side of her open sleeping pod, turning to where she had left off. She read until Ephraim returned.

"The screen says we're down twenty-five people. Wonder who? Wonder what happened to them? Suppose they headed out last night?"

"Who knows. I'm tired of trying to keep count. Come on – let's go to the dispensary. I'm hungry."

Bailey and Ephraim walked down the narrow, domed metal corridor to the food dispensary: a circular, domed metal room, perhaps thirty feet in diameter, with sliding metal doors -- food stations -- mounted flush in the walls at thirty-six-inch intervals around the circumference. Stainless steel tables and benches filled the center of the room. Each food station had a small touch-activated menu and payment screen that, like everything else, only worked when the sun was up. All of the food stations had lines of people-Bailey and Ephraim took up places in separate lines next to one another. They waited silently for their turn, as did everyone: conversation was frowned upon while in line for rations.

The two had agreed to allocate no more than three credits per meal-they were allotted two hundred twenty-five credits per person per month, but credits were also needed for other things, like laundry, personal hygiene products, and taking out library books. Over the past three months they had managed to save fifteen credits.

Both purchased the same meal: oatcakes with eggs and coffee. Not that the oatcakes were made from cultivated oats, or that the eggs were laid by real chickens. Most food was manufactured in underground cavern laboratories. Nutritional counts were strictly formulated. There were no obese people in this shelter: there was no one with lifestyle-induced heart disease, hypertension, high levels of cholesterol, or diabetes. And no one left any food on their plates.

"Finished? We've got five minutes to check in at the gym. We'd better hurry – we don't want demerits for being late." Bailey picked up both her and Ephraim's trays and took them to the dishwashing station.

Ephraim and Bailey checked into the gym in the nick of time. They first went to the health monitoring stations, where their weight, vitals, and blood chemistry were analyzed and recorded.

"Hey, Bales! We're only three acceptable monitoring events from earning massages!" That was a treat reserved for those that hit all of their individual health markers every day for six months.

The two took to their prescribed workouts, each hitting their heart rate markers, their lung capacity markers, and their blood oxygen marker. Each marker, when met, was recorded and displayed on an overhead screen, along with a flashing green light. New shelter residents learned very quickly that not meeting markers was a bad idea: the overhead screen flashed red, a very irritating alarm sounded, and a mild electric shock was delivered. It was thus that virtually every resident earned biannual massages.

Ephraim and Bailey's workouts lasted ninety minutes. They then went together into the antiseptic/cooling chamber, and sixty seconds later they came out refreshed, cool, and dry.

"What are you doing between now and lunch? I was thinking I would like to finish reading the book I borrowed."

Ephraim pushed the door open, letting Bailey go first. "I thought I would go to the cycling simulator. I'd like to ride through the old countryside."

"I'll meet you back at the sleeping pod at noon, then. If you need me, I'll be in the reading room." Bailey headed to their sleeping pod to grab her book. She called over her shoulder, "See you at lunch."

Bailey loved the classics. She was currently reading *Wuthering Heights*. She loved imagining being able to run through the moors, heavy clothing notwithstanding. She loved to imagine the freedom of wilderness… the freedom of unfettered space and open fields; of rain, of grass and trees and friendly sun.

Bailey curled up in her favorite reading room nook and finished the few chapters she had left to read: it didn't take her long to end the tale of Heathcliff and his Catherine. She sat with the book on her lap, pondering a society that would allow such relationships and behaviors. It was so utterly different back then. That's what kept her interested.

She took the book and returned it to the library. She started looking for other titles to borrow, but glancing at her watch, realized she needed to head back to the sleeping pod.

Ephraim snuck up behind her as she approached their sleeping pod. He put his hand on her waist and pulled her back a bit, leaning up against her and whispering in her ear.

"I reserved a sex pod at seven."

Bailey smiled and leaned back into him. "And how did you arrange that on such short notice?"

"I'll never tell." Ephraim nibbled on Bailey's ear. "But right now I could use some food." The two headed toward the food dispensary.

After a quick lunch, Bailey and Ephraim went to the garden to put in their mandatory gardening time. This week they were assigned to the potato section. The gardens were located in vast dirt caverns, with solar tubes providing bright light. The underground infrastructure collected brown water for irrigation. There were no weeds to pull: weeds had disappeared eons ago, and fertilization was handled via the recirculated brown water. Garden work meant planting, cultivating, and harvesting the few vegetable varieties adapted to being grown underground.

"Okay, Ephraim: why don't you harvest today? I'll plant seedlings behind you."

"Deal. I like this detail more than others, especially processing soy bacon. I 'm no fan of dealing with soy bacon."

"Me either. But we need to sign up for the soy bacon factory to get extra credits. Yeah – nasty. But we can manage it once a month, though, right?"

Ephraim and Bailey lived in Community A286, which was reserved for married couples under the age of forty with no children. There were several types of communities: B Communities were for singles under thirty; C Communities were for families with minor children and for those approved to have children; D Communities were for married couples over forty that did not have children; and E Communities were for people, married or not, age fifty-five and above. Individuals over the age of seventy who could not pass physical and mental tests were given the option of taking eternity pills or being sent to quiet, softly appointed -- but locked -- Centers to slowly starve to death with others in similar conditions. Medical comas were available to ease transition, and the remains of Center People were turned into fertilizer. People opting for eternity pills were turned out to the surface, as their remains were not suitable for fertilizer.

The year was 15862. The surface of the earth had long since gone arid and uninhabitable. Independent countries had disappeared centuries before, as had different races, customs, and languages. The human population had dwindled to only a few hundred thousand, as neither the earth nor the underground communities could support more than that. Pilgrim launches to other planets that could support human life had happened over the eons, and it was known that several had successfully landed on far away planets. Communication with them ceased hundreds and hundreds of years prior, however, as solar flares had long-since fried Earth's receivers. People on Earth could only hope the pilgrims were thriving in their new homes.

Ephraim and Bailey were both thirty-two. They met in Community B623 when they were twenty-eight, and their pairing was recommended by High Command based upon their DNA and brain chemistry. They were a very good match-the High Command rarely got their recommendations wrong. Everyone married and moved into A Communities before they turned thirty. Those who refused their chosen partner, or who didn't find a partner on their own prior to turning thirty, were denied credits for three months. If, after three months, they still refused High Command's mating recommendation and did not find a mate on their own, they were given the same options as those elderly residents that could not pass mental and physical tests.

Bailey and Ephraim resembled every other couple in many regards. Without sunlight, the human race had become fairer and fairer. Variation in height and facial features regressed toward the mean – every woman was between 5'6" and 5'10" tall; every man between 5'10" and 6'2". All jaws were on the square side; all noses were straight; all eyes wide set. All hair was straight and thin; all hair was blond or some lighter shade of red or brown. Everyone was mesomorphic. When power was more reliable, government identification had been made through biometrics. That method had become more and more unreliable as people started to resemble one another more and more. That fact, and increasingly strong and more frequent solar flares, drove High Command to mandate that all community uniforms must be embroidered with name and an individual identification number.

Ephraim and Bailey finished their garden duty and walked to the garden control unit. They signed out via touchscreen and headed to the cleaning room, where, sixty seconds later, they and their uniforms were disinfected, cleaned, and dried. Ephraim checked the information screen.

"6:45! Well, my dear-we need to skip dinner if we are to make our sex pod appointment."

Bailey grinned mischievously. "I've heard of sneaky ways to save credits, but this has got to be one of the best. After you, Sir Galahad."

"Sir Galahad?"

"You really need to read more, darling." Bailey took Ephraim's hand. "Come with me and let me tell you all about him."

~

Bailey and Ephraim checked into the sex pod. High Command had designed these chambers with the utmost care. They were the only chambers that were not perfectly sterile and utilitarian. The walls were covered in a velvety soft lavender fabric. The air was perfumed with muted lilac and lavender, and the center of the chamber was occupied by a large, old-fashioned mattress bed on a sleigh frame with sturdy head- and footboards. There were gauze curtains that hung from the ceiling, gathered and cinched at each corner with pale lavender velvet ties. The solar tube that provided light had a pink, partially translucent shade that removed the normal harsh glare. And on one wall was a small bar that held, for a price, two flutes with champagne and various assorted chocolate candies. A discreet cubby on the opposite wall held a variety of sex toys.

Bailey locked the door while Ephraim engaged the timer. Bailey walked up behind Ephraim, reached around him, and slowly started to unzip his uniform. Ephraim turned around, smiling. He stood back so Bailey could continue undressing him as he cupped her cheek in his hand and then nuzzled her neck. He stepped out of his uniform and proceeded to unzip hers. She stepped out of hers as it fell to the floor and the two headed towards the bed. The two were well-matched here, too: they both preferred slow, languid sex.

Afterwards, Ephraim rolled on his side, facing Bailey. "May I interest you in a flute of champagne?"

Bailey paused. "It costs too many credits, honey. And I was thinking... do you suppose we could start thinking of moving to a C community?"

Ephraim lay silent. "I suppose it's time to consider having children. I don't see a reason to wait. So that's why we are saving credits? To secure transportation to a C Community?"

"We have to fill out an application form and petition High Command – it's not like it will be tomorrow. But, yes, I think we're ready. I think it's time." Bailey kissed Ephraim.

"Too bad we can't toast our decision. But I agree; credits are too hard to save. We'll get an application form and file our petition tomorrow."

Just then their reservation timed out. The shade over the solar tube retracted and the pleasant scent was replaced with an antiseptic. Bailey and Ephraim quickly dressed and headed to their sleep pod.

CHAPTER TWO

Bailey and Ephraim appeared before the Community Administrative Board as ordered, in the matter of their petition to move to a C community.

"State your names?"

"Ephraim Josiahson, sir."

"Bailey Josiahson."

"Maiden name?"

"Fairchild."

The Board members scanned the petition as it appeared on their tablets.

"You were married October 28, 15860, correct?"

"Yes, sir." Ephraim answered for both of them.

"And you met in B286, right?"

"Yes, sir."

"We take it you are requesting a move to start a family?"

"Yes, sir. We believe we are ready."

There was a pause from the members of the Board as they scanned the couple's medical, credit, and demerit records.

"You realize that the move will cost you fifty credits."

"We understand, sir. We have accumulated fifteen so far. We should be able to accumulate the entire amount within three months."

The Chair paged through several documents before speaking again.

"Your medical and social records support a move at this time. We will assign you a space in C488. The shuttle for C488 departs November 18th. We can lend you the required additional credits, and you can repay them by a five-credit monthly deduction. Mrs. Josiahson, you will be granted leave from all manual labor in your third trimester.

The family unit will be given an additional credits monthly upon the birth of your first healthy child, as determined by the Community Medical Board. No additional credits or relief from duty assignments will be given if the Board does not certify the child. Do you agree to these terms?"

"We do, sir."

"You are approved to transfer. Starting tomorrow, you will receive your rations from a pending transfer – C food dispensary station."

Bailey spoke up. "Excuse me for asking, but I've always wondered how those rations are different?"

"They have higher percentages of anti-radiation additives and they are free of the birth control additive included in normal rations. Good luck to you two."

"Thank you, sir." Ephraim and Bailey left the boardroom. Once they got out into the hall they hugged each other excitedly. They disentangled immediately when a clerk approached them.

"There are forms for you to complete for the transfer. I'll send the link to your sleep pod screen. Please make sure the information is completed within forty-eight hours."

"We will. Thank you."

"Good luck. I hope your trip is uneventful. Shuttle schedules have been disrupted more and more with the increasing solar flares. Hopefully you won't be caught in one."

As they walked back to their sleep pod, Bailey spoke.

"Should we take soy bacon shifts to earn extra credits? And maybe we can skimp on food?"

"We can't skimp on food too much or our vitals will suffer. Maybe we can save an extra three or four credits between soy bacon shifts, making sure we take no high-credit food items, and putting off buying everything we can think of, but I doubt we can do better than that."

"I'm game if you are."

"The next three weeks might seem like forever, but let's give it a go."

~

Bailey and Ephraim managed to save additional credits over the following weeks, giving them a total of thirty-eight as they boarded the November 18th shuttle. They would need about thirty-five for food until December 1st, when the next allotment was distributed. They left for C488 with a forty-eight credit debt. The next several months would be tight.

They headed to the transport bay as soon as the sun provided light to the underground village. The transport bay was heating up rapidly as the sun hit the metal door that opened to the surface. Bailey and Ephraim joined the several other couples being checked in biometrically at the kiosk next to the stairs that led into the transport.

The shuttle held sixteen people. It consisted of a large, thin, domed protective shield that had tucked within it a blimp-shaped chamber meant for passengers. Solar panels on top of the shield provided power. The contraption traveled very slowly, hovering only inches above the surface of the earth – it had to be able to set down very suddenly in case of a wind or sandstorm; or if there was a blast of electrons from a solar flare; or if, for some reason, the solar panels were occluded and power was lost. The shuttles were engineering marvels: they managed a very delicate balance between keeping the air and temperature within the chamber habitable while mitigating the hostile environment, and the ever-present potential for excess radiation exposure – all with solar power and with no storage batteries. Given all of this, it was a very good idea to get to the next underground community as soon as possible.

Once the travelers were strapped into their seats, the bay was evacuated as a large ceiling panel slid open, allowing the sun to hit the transport's solar panels. The bay's metal exit door opened, and the transport raised up a few inches and slowly left the bay. Once the transport was clear, the metal door and the ceiling panel closed; they were on their way.

Community C488 was located in what used to be Ohio, however none of the passengers could be expected to know that: states and countries were relegated to far-gone history. High Command knew the locations of communities, but that information was not available to ordinary citizens.

"So, are you excited about going to a family community?" Ephraim asked the couple sitting across from Bailey and him. The woman smiled shyly and squeezed her husband's hand.

"We are – very. And you?"

"We're ready," said Bailey. "I was wondering: do either of you have any idea how long this trip will last?"

"No idea. Hopefully we won't be topside for too long. I am not keen on being exposed to surface conditions."

Conversation stopped momentarily as a robot came up and offered rations – a nondescript, thick cream-colored drink.

"My name is Bailey, and this is my husband, Ephraim."

"Nice to meet you. My name is Sarah, and this is my husband, Abraham."

Just then the transport shook and quickly settled down onto the surface dust.

"What's happening?"

A voice came over the PA system. "We have hit a dust storm. The power will dim, and may be extinguished until the storm has passed. Plea….." Static overtook speech, and then the voice was silenced, along with interior lights. Everyone was locked in place in total darkness, the automatic seat restraint releases locked by the pilot. Bailey quietly sipped her drink, slipping her left hand over to find Ephraim. He took her hand in his. The cabin fell silent.

Bailey finished her drink and drifted off to sleep. She awakened when the transport lit up and lifted off the surface.

"I must have drifted off. How long were we dormant?"

"A couple of hours, I think."

The automatic seat restraints unlocked as a voice came over the PA. "The storm has passed. You are free to move about the transport. If we need to set down again, please find the nearest available seat and sit down immediately."

"Honey, I'm going to make a quick trip to the lav." Bailey got up and walked towards the back of the transport. After using the facilities, she washed her face and hands. She stared at herself in the mirror. She saw a young woman with close-cropped, thin, straight, light brown hair. She contemplated her blue-green eyes; she was fairly indistinguishable from the majority of women in their thirties in the Communities. She sprayed her mouth with tooth maintenance solution and then went into the body and clothes compartment. Sixty seconds later she and her uniform were clean and disinfected. She went back to the mirror one last time. She briefly thought of Jane Eyre. *I can't imagine changing clothes!* She tugged at her tunic to straighten it and headed to her seat but changed her mind and headed for the reading material rack. She found no classics. Disappointed, she picked up a history of the founding of the High Command and headed back to Ephraim.

The transport suddenly jerked and landed abruptly before Bailey made it back to her seat. She grabbed the nearest empty seat and buckled herself in. She ended up across from a sleeping man who was not awakened by the jostle. Several seconds later the transport was thrown again into darkness... there wasn't even time for an announcement over the PA. With little else to do, Bailey closed her eyes and relaxed, letting her thoughts float, drifting into a half-sleep. She dreamt she was back in the 1800's. She had long hair and petticoats, a corset, and a bonnet. She was outside, on a lovely green hill, when she saw Ephraim in the distance. He was a silhouette against a rising sun. She started toward him, smiling, her petticoats and skirts pleasantly rusting against the grasses and wildflowers at her feet. She bent down to pick a few flowers, but when she stood back up, Ephraim was no longer standing. The sun was no longer friendly – it had started to rage. The dewy grass and flowers turned brown within seconds and the ground dried up. She saw Ephraim crumple into a heap on the ground where he had stood. She started to run to him, but the wind was blowing strongly against her, picking up sand and hurling it at her. It stung her face so badly she had to turn away.

Bailey woke with a start. She shook her head to clear it. The transport was still in total darkness, huddled under its protective shell. Bailey strained to hear whether it was a sandstorm, but the transport and the shell were very well insulated. She began breathing deep, regular breaths and started tensing then relaxing her muscles, beginning at her feet and working her way up to her forehead. She concentrated on her breathing and her muscle relaxation, and then focused on listening to her heartbeat. She fell into a dreamless, restful sleep, only awakening when Ephraim shook her shoulder. The lights were back on and the transport was underway.

"Pleasant sleep?"

Bailey quickly got up and headed back with Ephraim. "I am so very glad we're underway again. Do you know what happened?"

"It was a sandstorm, of apparently epic proportion. It lasted several hours. I missed having you next to me in the dark." Ephraim gave Bailey a hug before sitting down.

"Have you heard how long we'll be on the surface?"

"Apparently C488 is two days away. I don't know how much time we lost, but hopefully we'll be safely underground again in a couple of days."

"Won't be soon enough." Bailey sat down, buckled in, and picked up the book she borrowed.

~

There were several more sudden groundings before the transport reached C488, three full days after leaving A286. When the transport was safely in the landing bay and the exterior doors closed, the transport exit door opened, and the weary travelers arrived at their new home.

"These communities all look alike, don't they?" Bailey said as she walked out of the landing bay and into the corridor.

"There have to be some differences inside. This one has to have schoolrooms, nurseries, and delivery rooms."

At the end of the corridor stood the Director of New Admissions. The travelers queued up, waiting their turn to be told their pod assignments and to have their remaining credits entered into the C488 system.

Ephraim and Bailey had no problem locating their assigned sleep pod – all of the communities had the same basic layout. They unlocked the door and immediately turned on the information screen. A scrolling banner that took up most of the screen started its continuous loop, from right to left.

Welcome to Community C488. We hope your needs will be met. You will notice a few differences between B and C communities. The nursery and maternity ward is situated next to the exercise area. The children's learning center is to the left of that. C Communities are larger than all others because of these extra areas. You are required to check into the medical center within the next twenty-four hours so we can confirm medical records and determine your fertility schedule.

Non-conformance will result in penalties…. Welcome to Community C488. We hope your needs…"

Ephraim turned off the information screen. "I wonder how long that message is going to loop?" He turned to Bailey.

"I really think a trip to the exercise facility is a stellar idea. After three days in that transport I could use a good workout."

"Couldn't agree more. Let's go!" Bailey jumped up and followed Ephraim as he opened the door.

Ephraim checked in to the vitals station and was pleased to see that his history had already transferred. He was ready to leave but saw a red alarm on the screen: *Record incomplete. Sperm count not recorded. Visit medical center prior to commencing exercise regimen.* Bailey got a similar message: *Fertility cycle not established. Visit medical center prior to commencing exercise regimen.*

"Well, I guess I know where we're headed." Ephraim stood by the door, letting Bailey exit before following her to the medical center.

By the time the two had finished their medical review it was time to eat. They headed to the food dispensary. The area looked much like the one they had used before, except that there were differentiated stations: special stations for pregnant and lactating women, for children between the ages of three and seven, for children between the ages of eight and puberty; for post-pubescent girls, for post-pubescent boys, and for everyone else. It was impossible to stay in line at an incorrect station – scanners identified age and condition and would alarm if a resident queued in the wrong line. The scanners were so effective that frequently it was the first indication that a woman was pregnant.

After eating, Ephraim and Bailey went back to the exercise facility. This time they were permitted to exercise. They completed their prescribed routines and returned to their pod. Bailey turned on the information screen, but the lights flickered, and static disrupted the message.

"Must be another damned solar flare," muttered Bailey. "I think I'll go to the library and see what I can find."

Bailey got as far as two doors down – the lights flickered several times before going out entirely. Bailey turned around and felt her way back to her pod. She pounded on the door a couple of times and called out to Ephraim.

"Ef, can you please manually open the door?" After a few moments the door opened, and Bailey walked in.

It was pitch black, except for the small, phosphorescent minerals that could hold light for several minutes before going dark themselves that were embedded in the walls above the head of each sleep pod.

"Is it just me, or are these blackouts becoming worse?"

"Let's not think about it, Bales. The night is young, we are alone.... What say you join me on the floor?" Ephraim nuzzled Bailey's neck as he reached to unfasten her uniform. Bailey smiled in the dark.

"That's the whole purpose of this community, isn't it? I think it's our civic duty."

~

The underground village remained dark until the next morning. It was the longest outage either Ephraim or Bailey had ever experienced.

"That must have been one hell of a sandstorm. Typhoon strength."

Bailey turned on the information screen. The screen was snowy with static, but the scrolling was at least legible.

We recently experienced a major sandstorm in conjunction with a significant solar flare. Services may be intermittent. Surface weather stations are down. Food rations: 421 days....... Shelter headcount........ 2,435.......... Change from yesterday.......... +4

.... Interior air quality............. 89%................. Next scheduled receipt of supplies................ 96 days.................... Medicine stock status..................... 82 days .... Radiation index............. high........................ Sunspot activity..................... high............ Night travel advisory....... Significant windstorm possible for next 36 hours........ Your schedule for today...... Exercise regimen...0900 hours......... potato garden........ 1300 hours..... sex pod....... 1600 hours........ fertility timing......... optimum........... Food rations: 421 days........

"Have you noticed, Ef? Stocks of rations and medical suppliers are less than at A286. And air quality is lower, too."

Ephraim took a minute to read the scrolling messages.

"That makes sense, because the time until the next receipt of supplies is less, too. And I imagine the sandstorm has a lot to do with the decreased air quality. I think that it will bounce back within a few days."

Bailey checked the time. "We have time for a quick breakfast before making our exercise window. We'd better get going."

After eating and exercising, Bailey went to the library and perused the available titles. There was not much in the classics section, and most of what was on the shelves she had already read. *Jane Eyre. Dante's Inferno. Le Compte de Monte Cristo.* She then noticed a title she had never seen: *On the Beach.* Bailey picked it up and flipped it over, but the back cover was blank. Deciding something new was better than re-reading anything, she checked it out and took it back to her pod... she had a full five hours for lunch and reading before her mandatory shift in the potato garden. She looked at the book and marveled that someone, long ago, had the prescience to place these ancient stories onto indestructible material. They needed no power: they just needed light. Bailey loved books. She started reading and was soon adrift in a world where Australia and submarines existed.

"Ef, do you ever wonder what our lives would be like if we lived when people were above ground?"

"Umm... not really."

"Do you think that oceans still exist?"

"No idea, babe."

Frustrated, Bailey curled up once again with her book. Since it was obvious that her husband did not share her fascination with what used to be, she once again got lost in the past. Ephraim turned on the information screen.

Food rations: 381 days....... Shelter headcount........ 2,435.......... Change from yesterday.......... 0 .... Interior air quality............. 85%................. Next scheduled receipt of supplies................ 82 days......................Medicine stock status...................... 70 days .... Radiation index.............. high........................... Sunspot activity...................... high............. Night travel advisory....... Significant windstorm possible for next 36 hours........

The screen then went white with static, although the lights were still on.

"Must be another solar flare," Ephraim muttered as he turned off the screen and turned to Bailey. "Bales, do you recall the inventory stats from when we got here?"

"They were lower than our B Community, I recall. I just can't remember by how much."

"I think they're down again, but I can't be sure."

"Maybe a supply shuttle got delayed. I haven't heard of any issues. I wouldn't worry about it." Bailey put down her book. "I'm bored. Think we can get into a virtual pod and take a hike up a mountain before dinner?"

"Sure, babe. Good idea."

The virtual pod located in the exercise facility, which always required health readings prior to use.

Bailey Josiahson... age 32 years, 69 days, twelve hours, 36 minutes..... height 5' 8", weight 130 pounds... blood pressure 115 over 75... blood chemistry within range. Clear to exercise, no limitations.

"Ef – this is strange. It yesterday it gave me information on my menstrual cycle. That's missing."

"Maybe that last solar flare damaged the reader."

Ephraim Josiahson... age 32 years, 116 days, three hours, sixteen minutes... height 6'1", weight 185 pounds, blood pressure 112 over 72, blood chemistry within range. Clear to exercise, no limitations.

"Must be that reader... my sperm count isn't listed, either. Strange. Oh well... let's go climb a mountain."

The couple chose to climb Mount McKinley. This was one of their favorite exercises... the 3D surround images, which were connected to floor plates that inclined to match the images, were exhilarating. The domed ceiling displayed blue skies and fluffy clouds, and the chamber was scented with "fresh air." A special solar tube mimicked the actual sun – how it used to be, when people inhabited the surface.

The two climbed until they reached a small, grassy vale. Now the scent changed to grass. They sat down on a couple of "rocks" and enjoyed the scenery, as a pair of moose wandered by. An eagle soared overhead, and songbirds could be heard coming from a stand of aspen.

Bailey sighed in satisfaction. "Ah, this is the life."

Just as they were starting to stand, their session ended. The floor settled back to flat, the screen images went black, and they were back in a sterile, empty chamber. They looked at each other, shrugged, and checked out.

"That's my favorite, Ef. I wish I could have lived back then."

"We'll come back soon, Bales. Maybe we can try Kilimanjaro. Or Etna! That might be an experience."

They headed back to their pod.

"You know Ef, this book is interesting. It's about nuclear war which sends clouds of deadly radiation across the globe, killing whole populations. There's a captain of a submarine that falls in love with a woman in a place called Australia, where the radiation hasn't reached. I need to see if I can find out where Australia was. Strange that there were separate countries fighting one another back then. That's what submarines were built to do. Wage war."

"Still want to live back in time?" Ef grinned and poked her. "Want to see a war?"

"Silly." Bailey turned away from his poke but grinned back at him. "Hmmm – five o'clock. Let's go get some supper. How are we doing on credits?"

"We can make it until distribution day if we stay at two credits each for breakfast and three each for lunch and dinner. Paying back that loan isn't easy, but we'll manage."

"Ah... to once again be able to buy dessert! That is my goal, Ef – a dessert!"

"You have modest goals, my sweet." Ephraim kissed her on the cheek. "Let's go."

As they walked, Bailey started again. "I wonder what the surface looks like in other places. Are there places where people can still live above ground? We never hear about other places, do we? And the world is a pretty big place. I wonder if our communities are all connected and are everywhere, or if there are separate 'countries' that have their own, different systems."

"That's my Bales. You certainly wonder a lot. Must be all of those books."

"And unfortunately, I think I've read every classic in the library. I have no idea what I'll do for an encore."

"Take care of a baby?"

"Hopefully. But we aren't pregnant yet. I thought we might be by now."

"Patience, love. Patience." Ephraim opened the dispensary door and let Bailey pass.

As they stood in their respective lines, the screens went snowy, the solar tubes darkened, and the food dispensary doors froze in position. There was a general grumbling among the residents. After several minutes the situation did not improve, and about a quarter of the residents left their queues. Some waiting children began to squabble and others started to run around, playing chase.

"Damn – must be another solar flare on top of a dust storm. Bales, let's go. We can come back later. I am sure they'll open the dispensary after things settle down on the surface." Bailey nodded but said nothing, and the two departed.

"I'm hungry, Ef. Maybe we should try and buy a little bit more every day and stash it back in our pod. These interruptions are irritating."

"You know that is against the rules."

"So is not eating. This community seems so less stable than the last. Think it's the location? I wonder what country this land would have been in."

Their conversation was interrupted by a knock on the door. Outside stood a couple of men with a rolling cart loaded with food.

"Power to the dispensary operations has been compromised, so we've been instructed to distribute emergency rations. We're sorry, but choice of foods has been eliminated. Here are your dinners. The credit system has temporarily been disabled: you will not be charged for your rations, but you will not be given your credit allotment for deliveries made, either."

"What about other things we might need?"

"If there are non-food essentials you require, the administration will be taking requests every Tuesday morning between one and four in the afternoon."

Ephraim took the plates. "What's going on?"

"We wish we knew. We were only given these instructions. Hopefully things will get back to normal soon."

The men with the cart started to leave, but Bailey spoke up.

"What time will you be delivering food tomorrow?"

"We'll be here with breakfast at 0800, and lunch at 1300. We haven't gotten instructions past that."

"That's a good sign. Thanks."

Bailey closed the door as the men rolled their cart to the next pod.

"Sounds like a temporary issue."

"If it's temporary, I don't know why they changed the credit system. Something's not right, Bales." Bailey had never heard concern in Ephraim's voice before.

"I've never heard you sound worried before, Ef."

"I've never been in a situation like this before. Something's not right." He sat down on the edge of his sleep pod with his plate. Sleep pod chambers were never designed for eating, and none had tables.

"Well, at least the food looks normal. Like something I would normally order." There were potatoes – there were always potatoes – mixed with spinach and soy bacon. Bailey had the same.

The dust storm must not have been dense, because there still was some light that got through. The two ate in silence.

"Wonder what we're supposed to do with these plates. Those men didn't say."

"I'll take them to the dispensary. Maybe the cleaning stations are open." Bailey reached over to take Ephraim's plate and headed out the door. "Be back soon."

The food dispensary seemed farther away in the dimly lit hallway. The dispensary door was partially open, and Bailey squeezed in sideways. She looked around – she was amazed at how sullen the room looked when totally vacant, with no lines or lit screens. The door to one cleaning station was halfway open, but the surface behind it was full of dirty dishes. She looked in, and tilting her arm upward, managed to place her two plates on top of the stack. She turned around, suddenly spooked. Everything seemed eerily abandoned. She hurried back to Ephraim.

"I think you are right, Ef. Something's just not right."

They sat across from one another, wondering what to do. Ephraim tried to turn on the information screen. It came on but was nothing but static snow.

"Well, we can't exercise, we can't go on a virtual hike – or sail, or ski, or anything else."

"There are always books, Ef. If you sit under the solar tube, there's enough light to read. Come to the library with me."

"Well, that's better than sitting around doing nothing. You'll make a reader out of me yet."

They left their sleep pod and entered the dim hallway. The hallways were mostly abandoned. They passed many pod doors with food trays littering their stoops.

"You know, Ephraim, I think as you get into the way things used to be you'll be fascinated. How very different lives were back then!"

"So you've said."

"Don't be such a grump. It's a marvelous way to expand your horizons and get to imagine another way of life."

When they got to the library the doors were open, but the place was empty. The kiosk for checkout was down – there was no way to record a check-out. Bailey and Ephraim looked at each other, shrugged, and started looking at titles.

"Here Ef, I think you might really like this one." She picked up *The Hobbitt.* "This is a fantasy series – this is the first. It's basically a tale of good versus evil, and it has all sorts of magic and fantastical creatures. I think you'd find it engaging."

Ephraim looked at the front and the back. Without an alternative activity, he decided to give it a go.

Bailey looked around for herself. She wasn't done with *On the Beach* but knew she would be soon. She skimmed past all of the titles she had already read but stopped at *Atlas Shrugged.*

"Here's one I haven't read before. This the first time I've seen it – perhaps it's just very popular." She picked it up.

"Let's find some light."

They left and headed toward the community room. It had the best lighting in the community and had comfortable chairs in the reading nook. This room was also strangely empty – only a few other people.

"Wonder where everybody is?" Bailey asked rather absent-mindedly as she found a chair directly under a solar tube. The light filtering through was dirty yellow and dim. "Must be some sandstorm."

The two sat and read until the light became too dim. They headed back to their sleep pod, feeling their way through hallways that were nearly pitch black. Ephraim ran his hand lightly down the walls, counting doors until they got to theirs.

"I think we missed supper."

"I think you're right. I'm surprised they didn't leave our food by the door."

"Maybe they did, and someone took it," said Ephraim as he unlocked and manually slid the pod door open. They stumbled in through the black.

There was an awkward silence as Bailey and Ephraim sat, not tired but with nothing to do in the dark. Finally Ephraim got up and headed toward the door.

"I'm going down to the administration quadrant to see what I can learn about what's happening."

"Go with you?"

"No. Probably better if you stay here. Maybe food delivery is late. I'll be back as soon as I can." Ephraim closed the door behind him.

Bailey closed her eyes and in her mind, headed back to favorite passages from memorable books. She was Claire Randall Fraser, time traveler, moving through the rocks between worlds. She imagined her boots wet and cold with mud. She wiggled her toes. She tried to imagine rain driving against her huddled, blanketed body, but had nothing to compare it to. Wet. She poured a little water into her cupped hand and splashed it into her face. *Maybe like that.* She imagined the sun beating down on her as she planted... planted peas. Yes, peas. They were round and green and grew in pods that needed to be broken open. She wondered how they tasted. And apples and pears and other tree-borne fruits. There were so many foods that she had read about but couldn't taste. Couldn't *imagine* the taste. She leaned back and imagined herself running in tall grass on a flat plain; gentle breeze, warm sun, chirping birds. A deer in the distance. Some fluffy clouds overhead. Long hair, in a braid. A straw hat. Petticoats and button-up boots. A lace umbrella, just for show. She smiled in the dark. She would have been so happy there. She wished only for enough light to once again lose herself in another time.

No longer able to read her book, she drifted off to sleep lost in her imagined lives before Ephraim returned.

~

Ephraim felt his way down the blackened hall. There were a couple of turns he needed to make to get to the administration quarters, but he knew the route well. He was surprised to see a dim light coming through the partially open door of the control room. He heard voices raised in animated argument. He paused, out of range of the light spilling through the portal.

"You didn't tell me that you were going to feed people poison to see who, if any, would be strong enough to go with us to Silo Six."

"I didn't believe you had a need to know."

"How many people are not ill or dead?"

"Apparently a few. Most residents are simply ill; maybe a few dozen died. Weak constitutions. Wouldn't have survived the journey anyhow. We don't have a count of how many are immune. There are a couple dozen pairs that have not answered for food distribution; we don't know if they are simply elsewhere or are unconscious in their rooms. There are some, definitely, who are still well enough to return their food trays."

"Shall we force open all doors?"

"Not enough power to do that. And we don't want to raise suspicion."

"What are we doing to our community? This is… this is simply immoral! Are we just going to leave the sick to die? Are we not at least going to give them end choices?"

There was a tense silence in the room.

"How many agree with Commander Jones?"

Of the couple dozen commanders assembled, only three hands went up. Major General Pinnock spoke. "You three are welcome to take your eternity pills. That, or support the plan and go with us to Silo Six."

There was dead silence in the room. The two hands raised late were lowered. Commander Jones bit his lip, looked at his fellow officers, and then held out his hand.

"I cannot in good conscience agree to murder. Please give me my eternity pill. I'd rather die with these innocents than live with the shame."

"It will be served with your last meal. Thank you for your service." Major General Pinnock was cold and curt.

Ephraim heard enough. He slowly and silently stepped backwards, further into the black, and when he reached the first turn he hurried back to his pod.

"Bailey. Wake up."

Bailey woke with a start. Ephraim's voice was low and his tone urgent.

"What? What's wrong?"

Ephraim felt his way over and sat down next to her on the edge of her sleep pod.

"It was pitch black by the time I got to the Admin quadrant. The door to the main room was open, and somehow they had some light. I have no idea how. I stopped near the door because there was a heated argument going on. No one noticed me.

"The administration was arguing about poisoning this community. It's a good thing we missed that food distribution: the food was tainted. High Command is heading out on a shuttle from some 'Silo Six' and is abandoning Earth. One Commander has chosen to take his eternity pill instead of leaving. He couldn't stand the guilt."

"Where is everybody else? Do you know?

Ephraim paused. "Most are ill – still taking in their food trays but not leaving their pods. A few dozen, apparently, have already died. I think those that are immune to the poison will go with Command on the shuttle. That's why there's nearly no one around. I don't think we are the only ones not affected, but not even High Command knows exactly. Not enough power to force open all doors."

Bailey's hand clutched Ephraim's in terror.

"Oh my God, Ef. Oh my God."

Ephraim paused and then very quietly spoke.

"I don't know when the shuttle is leaving."

"What and where is Silo Six?"

"That's what I am going to find out. Until then, we need to go to the gardens and pick our own food. Potatoes and spinach, I guess, will have to do."

WENDY SURA THOMSON

CHAPTER THREE

Bailey and Ephraim made sure to be out of their pod for two meals out of three. They did accept one meal a day, promptly throwing out the food and returning the empty trays to the food dispensary. They made sure to weigh themselves down with whatever they could find to outwit the health center diagnostics. For all practical purposes it appeared they were perfectly immune to what had been added to the rations. They saw fewer and fewer people – except for three other couples that showed up in the gardens regularly. Bailey and Ephraim ate right from the garden, making sure to not rinse anything in water, scraping off the dirt from the potatoes as best they could, and using their fingernails to peel off as much skin as they could manage. The eight people in the garden never spoke to one another – they merely eyed each other with distrust. After two weeks, two Commanders showed up in the garden.

"Please, all of you – come with us."

Bailey glanced at Ephraim as she put down her basket of potatoes. She brushed her hands onto her work apron, then took it off. Everyone filed out between the Commanders; one leading and one picking up the rear. They were shepherded into the Command Center, where sixteen of the community's leaders stood waiting.

Major General Pinnock, standing on a small platform, spoke.

"I want to congratulate you on the strength you have shown in tolerating the additives that were mixed into your rations. Very few in the community have your resilience. It is for that reason that you have been invited to head to Silo Six with us to board the last outgoing shuttle."

There was a concerned murmuring in the small crowd.

"As you may have surmised, conditions in this community have significantly deteriorated. Our power systems are unable to sustain us, and have furthermore degraded communications to such a degree that we cannot determine whether other communities equally affected. Supply deliveries have been irregular, and we are dangerously low on many necessary items, especially medical supplies."

"Where is the shuttle headed?" A voice called out from the crowd.

"We'll be heading toward the closest colony with which we have had the most recent communication. This voyage is not assured of success, but High Command has determined that we either take the chance and leave or face certain extinction here."

A woman broke down sobbing and suddenly bolted toward Pinnock, screaming in fury and pain.

"My children are gravely ill in the medical center. You're telling me it was the additives? It was you? You *poisoned* my children? You monster!!! How can you live with yourself? You… you..." Her husband attempted to hold her back and console her, with no success.

"No!" She pulled away and dashed toward Pinnock but was stopped by a couple of officers.

Major General Pinnock's glared at the sobbing woman and his voice became icy and stern. "Stay with your children, then. Bradshaw, give this woman her eternity pill. Take them, or not. Starve to death, if you wish. Or fall asleep forever. Also give her husband his pill, and a pill each for their children. Oh – and Bradshaw, distribute eternity pills to everyone in the medical center and leave two by every sleep pod door. And leave a pile on the first table in the food dispensary. People will figure it out soon enough."

"What should we say about the pills, sir?"

"Nothing. Just leave them."

Bradshaw and another administrator took the couple, who were now struggling with them, out of the Command Center. The remaining couples, dumbfounded, were silent.

"Any other complaints?" Pinnock paused for several moments as he looked down on the civilians standing in front of him. "Fine then. Be at the landing bay tomorrow at first light."

Ephraim and Bailey were uncharacteristically quiet that night. But as they lay in the pitch black, each in their sleep pods, Bailey's voice rose and cut through the black velvet of night.

"Ef?"

"Yes, babe?"

"Suppose I can bring a book or two?"

CHAPTER FOUR

Neither Bailey or Ephraim slept that night. When the first trace of light hit the solar tube and bounced into the pod, they were up. They had nothing to bring with them except the two books they borrowed from the library and the clothes on their backs.

"If I make a mad dash, do you 'spose I can grab a couple more books?"

Ef stopped and considered. Normally he would have said no, but understanding Bailey, he said, "Go! And run! You must be at the landing bay when I get there. Don't even worry about what you grab – pick anything and run, Bailey. Don't browse!"

Bailey sprinted to the library, grabbed the first few books she came across, and sprinted to the landing bay. She met Ephraim twenty feet short of the portal. They entered together, hand in hand.

The transport was sitting in the bay with its shell lifted and its gangway out. The cadre of Commanders and administrators were already there, but Ephraim and Bailey were the first couples to board. They took seats in the back, away from the others. Bailey tucked the books under her seat. A few minutes later Major General Pinnock entered and looked around.

"We're missing two couples. Carew! Oglethorpe! Go round them up." Carew and Oglethorpe left as ordered. They returned in ten minutes, alone.

"Sir, we can't locate them."

Pinnock checked the control panel. "Leave them then. We need to depart. Lock down the hatch, open the bay and engage transport." The hatch shut, the protective shell lowered and locked on to the shuttle, and the transport rose to hover. The bay doors slowly parted and the transport slowly floated out over the surface.

"Don't bother closing the transport bay doors."

Pinnock turned to Ephraim and Bailey. "You two are future, you know? The only fertile pair left from C488. In fact, you, madam, are the only fertile woman on board." Ephraim felt a knot in his stomach. He instinctively leaned towards Bailey and wrapped an arm around her.

Pinnock continued. "You are matched, which is lucky for you. I hope that the B leaders bring dozens of young women for the rest of us." Nervous laughter rose up from the administrators.

"We were tasked by High Command to bring the best with us in hopes of keeping the species alive. You'll get the best we have to offer during transport. That's why we allowed you to steal those books under your seat."

Pinnock turned to Bradshaw. "Bradshaw, head us east northeast, heading 285."

"Aye sir."

Pinnock turned to Ephraim and Bailey. "Hungry?"

There were very quick denials from both. Pinnock laughed. "If you're worried about the food supply, don't be. Oglethorpe, bring in breakfast."

In short order, trays of biscuits, eggs, berries, and bacon were brought in. Bailey looked at the berries and eggs quizzically.

"Berries and eggs, my dear. Reserved for administration. You'll like them, I guarantee." Pinnock was filling his plate with them as he spoke. "Quite delicious."

Ephraim cautiously took a berry and popped it in his mouth. His eyes opened a bit wider. "Bales – try these! They are wonderful!" He followed Pinnock's lead and filled his plate. After he, Pinnock and Bailey had taken what they wanted, the rest of the crew lined up to eat.

"Glad you liked the food," said Pinnock, wiping his mouth and placing his empty plate back on the tray. "We have some old board games and cards that might interest you. It's going to be a rather long trip. That, or read. We have other books on board, if you want. You have a private pod – right next to mine." Pinnock walked to the starboard side of the transport, where there were two doors. "The first is mine. That's yours," he said, pointing to the door aft.

Ephraim and Bailey made their way back to the seats where they had stowed their books, picked them up, and went to their pod. They looked around with some amazement after opening the door. It was nothing like the pods they had in the communities. It was small, of course, but it was well-appointed. Instead of separate sleep pods it had one larger pod for the two of them. The floor was carpeted in a soft gray plush. The sleep pod's back was on an angle for reading and it had soft pillows and a chenille coverlet: a floral pattern, in soft gray and pale yellow. The pillows were stuffed into pale yellow cases. The walls appeared to be covered in a soft gray and pale yellow striped velvet. Hung conveniently on a wall near the sleep pod was a bed tray.

"Wow! Did you ever imagine that things like this existed?" Bailey said.

"Never thought about it. And no, I didn't."

Bailey clambered into the pod, fluffed a pillow behind her back, and leaned back on the comfortably angled wall. She wiggled down a bit and smiled. "This is great! Come try it."

Ephraim grabbed a couple books and joined Bailey. He bent his legs, leaned a book against his thighs, and opened it. "I could get used to this."

Bailey suddenly became pensive. "You know, there are two other doors on the other side of the transport. I bet they're pods just like this. They were supposed to be for those other two couples that never made it. But there is only room for three couples. I think one of the four that were called together yesterday would have been left behind one way or the other."

211

"Do you feel guilty?"

"A bit. Doesn't seem fair, does it?"

"We had nothing to do with what happened, Bales. Sometimes it's just the luck of the draw. We're here now, and that's all that matters."

Bailey sat silently for a bit, thinking about the situation, then she grabbed the top-most book from the stack.

"You're right, Ef. Nothing either you or I did had anything to do with the other couples. I think I'll get lost in a book." She turned the book to read the spine. "*One Thousand and One Nights.* This should be interesting." She opened it and quickly went back in time.

~

"General Pinnock, how much longer until we reach Silo Six?" The transport had been underway for two weeks and had to land several times a day due to adverse surface and weather conditions.

"Depends on conditions. We've not been fortunate in that regard, but things could change. We just swung out of a Maunder Minimum, and adverse activity soars at this point in the cycle."

Bailey was getting bored. She finished several books, learned how to play an ancient game called Euchre and had run six miles a day on the only piece of exercise equipment available in the transport. She sighed and looked around to see what else she could do.

"General, there are some blips on the sensors. Three objects are heading toward us. And they're not transports – transports can't move that fast."

Pinnock headed over to the screen and watched briefly as three objects closed in on them. They were coming in from three different directions, equally spaced.

"Lower the transport and engage the panel protectors." Pinnock turned to the Josiahsons. "We'll go black in several seconds in order to redirect all received energy to defensive batteries. Go into your pod and close the door. I'll engage lockdown shortly."

Ephraim took Bailey by the hand and pulled her into their pod. Seconds after he closed the door they heard the bolts and bars engage. Then it went dark.

They crawled into sleep pod and climbed in, then leaned back on the angled wall and listened. There were loud, unfamiliar thuds that sounded like something heavy repeatedly hitting the protective shell. Terse, animated conversation and orders bellowed out from the cockpit.

"Ever read *Treasure Island?*"

"Uh… nope. But that shouldn't surprise you, Bales."

"This reminds me of pirates."

"What's a pirate?"

"Pirates are – were – robbers and thieves that sailed on fast water ships, taking all that was worthwhile. Sometimes they let the sailors go. Sometimes they made them join the pirate crew. Sometimes they killed them."

"So you think we've been set upon by pirates?"

"I have no idea. This just reminds me of *Treasure Island.*"

Bailey sat quiet and listened to the repeating thuds. After a few moments Ephraim spoke.

"If so, then there are communities out there that were not part of High Command. And they have transports – or something – much faster than our transports. And where did that food we never saw before come from? We've lived in A, B, and C communities, and never saw any of that. There's got to be a world out there we have never seen."

The thuds grew louder, then they were interrupted by a very loud and high-pitched screech. The transport shook hard in a slow rhythm and then stopped moving altogether. There were many voices now – unfamiliar voices, giving orders. Ephraim clutched his arms around Bailey and held tight as the lights came on and the locks disengaged. The pod door opened, and there stood a short, muscular man – shorter than any community member by several inches. He had thick, cracked, dark, cinnabar-colored skin, very thick black hair, and near-black eyes with double lids. Neither Bailey nor Ephraim had ever seen anyone like him before. They instinctively leaned back against the wall.

"What have we here? By the looks of it, you are not crew. You are not administration… your uniforms tell me that. You must be civilians. What are you doing on an administration transport?"

"We were invited by Major General Pinnock."

"And where did Major General Pinnock tell you where you were going?"

"Someplace called Silo Six."

The man smiled. "That's not all you know, is it?"

Ephraim took the offensive. "And who are you? You are definitely not of a community."

The man smiled again. "So perceptive. I take it that High Command never told you about the other tribes."

Ephraim furrowed his brow. "What other tribes?"

"Not everyone went underground. We call ourselves the Kiwi. We live in Antarctica. We are descendants of people that once lived on islands called New Zealand. Wonder where those berries you ate came from? Us. We grow them. We have been trading with your High Command for centuries. As you can see, we adapted to the environment. Here…" he reached into his satchel. "You might want to take these. Iodine pills. Since we compromised your protective shell, these will come in handy. Iodine is the reason our skin is so dark." He handed a vial of pills to Ephraim.

"We are not here to harm you. The Earth is getting too hazardous for even us. We have noticed decimated communities on our trade routes. Something's going on. High Command has not been exactly forthcoming about the situation, so we decided to take it upon ourselves to find out what's been happening. And that's where folks like you come into the picture."

Ephraim looked at Bailey, questioningly. Ephraim gave the slightest nod. It was she who finally spoke.

"Yes, something's going on. We found out that additives were put into our rations. It made most very sick: some even died. There were only four couples that didn't get sick, and all were invited to come aboard. One couple had sick children who were going to be left behind and they became enraged when they learned the truth. They were escorted out. The other two couples were late getting to the landing bay, so we left without them. Eternity pills were left at everyone's door, and the landing bay door was left open to the elements. They left the entire community to die. There might be some who may survive for a while in the underground farms, but I don't know how long they'll last without supply deliveries. General Pinnock said that there's a rocket in Silo Six that will blast off to find a colony – hopefully. But he also said that that success is not assured."

The man listened patiently. "Thank you for confirming what we surmised. That High Command… they have always been such self-serving psychopaths. We always told them we should work together to survive. We have all sorts of technology that they don't: look at our transports. Far faster. We have evolved to accommodate environmental changes so much more effectively. What we don't have is a rocket. But no… High Command could not be convinced to work with us. Well, now they have no choice. We intend to be part of the exodus. We have no quarrel with you – you're very welcome to come along. As long as you agree to work with us."

Ephraim extended his hand. "I'm Ephraim. Ephraim Josiahson. This is my wife, Bailey."

The man took Ephraim's hand and shook it. "I'm Colonus. Captain Colonus. I recommend you remain in your pod. We're going to hitch this transport to ours and head for Silo Six – if we can convince your Major General to give us directions."

"If it helps, General Pinnock set a course at 285 degrees."

"Thank you. Very helpful indeed." Colonus turned to leave the pod.

"Oh – before you go: what do you Kiwis call us?" asked Bailey.

Colonus turned back to her and smiled.

"You? We call you Gophers." Colonus left, closing the door after him.

Soon after that, Ephraim and Bailey were knocked into their double-pod by a strong jerk as their transport was suddenly and quickly yanked by the three foreign transports – heading: 285 degrees.

Bailey turned to Ephraim. "What do you think of Colonus?"

"My first thought was, 'what else don't we know?' Do you trust him?"

"You know, I do. He seems genuine, and pretty open. What he said makes sense. Rather irksome that the administration has been trading with these people and keeping it all to themselves. I wonder what else they have that we don't."

"Ever hear about iodine helping with radiation exposure?"

"No."

"Me neither."

The two looked at each other, and then simultaneously took the iodine pills. Bailey continued. "Seems to have worked for Colonus and his tribe. Amazing how those folks adapted and lived. On the surface, no less. I am amazed."

"Gophers, huh? Strange name. 'Spose there are other tribes out there?"

"I imagine Colonus would know. We should ask him when we get the chance."

Bailey leaned back and licked her lips. "Those berries were delicious, weren't they? Can you imagine having those available? I wonder what else they grow in – where did he say – Antarctica?"

"We can ask him that, too. Maybe he'll bring along seeds so we can grow those wherever we end up."

There was a brief silence that Ephraim broke. "You know, Bales, if you had asked me this morning if I could ever imagine meeting someone from another tribe, that lived on the surface, that could travel much faster than us, and that's been trading with High Command for centuries, I would have thought that you'd gone off the deep end."

Bailey laughed. "I'm with you, there, Ef. What a strange turn of events. But, you know, I'm not afraid, for some reason, I'm not at all afraid of Colonus and his men."

"I'm not, either, Bales. I think it would be grand if we could sit down with him and have a long conversation. I bet it would be incredibly interesting."

"Suppose we could ask if we could have that conversation with one of his men? I'm dying to learn more."

"Maybe now is not the right time to ask. Maybe when we are all aboard the space shuttle. I imagine we'll have all sorts of time for long discussions. Hey – you read the history of the High Command. Was there anything at all in there about other tribes? Or trade?"

"Not a thing."

"Figures."

Just then their pod door opened and Colonus popped his head in.

"You can come on out now if you wish. Things are quiet out here, and we don't expect any issues."

"Any idea how long until we get to Silo Six?"

"Towing this transport is slowing us down a bit, but I imagine we'll arrive in three days or so. Pinnock was most cooperative when he understood that he would never get to his destination without cooperating with us."

"Does that three day timeframe include set-downs for bad weather?"

Colonus grinned. "It takes an awful lot for us to stop travel. In fact, I can think of only one time we were marooned for a while. Sandstorms do not affect us, and it takes a massive – and I mean *massive* – solar flare to disrupt our travel. Come on out: we've got food set up."

Ephraim and Bailey left their pod and walked out to the common area. The Command Center and pilot house were manned by Colonus's men. Pinnock, Bradshaw, Olgethorpe, and the rest were quarantined in a temporary seating area.

Colonus piped up, "Don't go near that seating area: there's a force field that surrounds it that is not very friendly to interference."

Pinnock glared out at Colonus and the Josiahsons.

Colonus ignored Pinnock, directing an order to one of his men in the Command Center.

"Latrelle, contact home base. Give them the coordinates of Silo Six. Tell them we should be arriving in thirty hours or so. Have the other transports in tow meet us there, and have them send several defensive units, just in case. We don't know whether word has gotten out or not."

"Didn't you say that we're all going leaving together?" asked Bailey.

Colonus turned to Bailey. "That would be my desire, but I'm not entirely certain your High Command is happy with that. You two, and any others that mean us no harm, are very welcome on board the shuttle. Truly. We can learn things from one another. If it doesn't turn out the way we want, it wasn't our doing."

"Sir, excuse me if this is not the right time, or inappropriate… but where you live: is it green?"

Colonus smiled. "There is still some green, but not nearly as much as there used to be. The water needed for trees and crops is rapidly drying up."

Bailey sighed. "That sounds wonderful. I read… I read a lot. I have read about green grasses and sitting under trees with shade from strong, wide branches. And oceans with waves, and little blue lakes. It all sounds so beautiful to me."

"You're quite the romantic, Mrs. Josiahson." Colonus smiled.

Ephraim stepped up next to his wife and smiled back. "That's one of her charms. Maybe not very practical, but charming." He leaned over and planted a small kiss on her head. Bailey scoffed it off.

"Well, you certainly didn't mind going into the hiking simulator and breathing in all of that simulated mountain air."

"Bales, we don't even know if that was based on reality. It may have been merely someone's fantasy."

Bailey didn't have a retort for that. It was true: what they thought was real had never been challenged.

General Pinnock had been listening to this chatter with obvious scorn. "You don't know how good you had it in the communities. You never had to build anything, defend anything, solve anything. You could simply live – the largest contribution you made was tending the gardens, and that wasn't much. And instead of appreciating it, you spent your time dreaming of what you didn't have. What a colossal waste. You never had it so good – and believe me: those good times have come to a screeching halt. You might regret not staying back and taking your eternity pills."

Colonus interjected. "Totally provided creature comforts bereft of the opportunity to work hard has robbed community members of a true sense of accomplishment. What did you leave them with? Few, if any, survival skills. A very limited understanding of mostly everything, from what I can see. They can read. Great. No wonder school only lasts a year for your children. When did you stop teaching math past basic arithmetic? Physics? Chemistry? And you obviously never taught geography or anything else at all, it would appear, except for completely biased version of High Command history."

That got Ephraim's attention. "Physics? Chemistry? There should have been classes for those? What are they?"

Pinnock smirked with shameless arrogance. "Oh, those subjects are taught. Just not to you common members. Those subjects are strictly for High Command and administration. You didn't need any of that, so it wasn't provided."

Colonus ignored Pinnock and answered Ephraim. "Physics and chemistry are areas of science. Physics studies the way things move and interact; how electricity moves, how communication networks function, how to build something so it will not collapse. Chemistry studies the composition of things; what things are made of, and how substances interact. Those two fields built your underground cities, provided energy for communications, designed your transports, and made your food and clothing."

Ephraim was shocked. He shook his head wistfully. "Man, that stuff is so interesting to me. I wish I knew… I wish I could have learned." He turned to Colonus. "I wish there had been some way to meet you sooner, sir. Somehow I think life would have been so much better."

Colonus turned to Latrelle. "Latrelle, you look around this transport and see if you can find any wiring diagrams or prints. I think that they might interest Mr. Josiahson."

Latrelle started going through all of the cubbies and storage areas of the Command Center. He finally found a maintenance and repair tablet and brought it to Colonus.

"Would this do?"

Colonus glanced at a few pages. "Yes, this is fine. Thank you, Latrelle." He held it out to Ephraim. "Here. This is not a textbook, but it might interest you. Latrelle, please answer any questions Mr. Josiahson might have."

"Yes, sir."

"Thank you so much, Captain Colonus. Would you mind if I took this into my pod?"

"Go right ahead." Ephraim headed towards his pod, his nose stuck in the tablet.

Bailey smiled. "I think now he understands my love of books." She turned to Colonus. "I would love to understand more of your world. Don't suppose you have a book or tablet about that?"

"No, not here. Sorry. But once we lift off on the shuttle we'll have more time than we know what to do with. I would be pleased to tell you what I know."

"That would be wonderful, and I look forward to it." Bailey turned towards the pod. "I am sure you are very busy. I think I need to grab a book and lose myself in it." Bailey took her leave.

~

In three short days the transport and her ferries found themselves in a large sea of transports – some ferried, some not. Colonus surveyed the mass of transports on the observation screen and turned to Pinnock.

"I assume from the crowd that we have arrived at Silo Six. General Pinnock, would you agree?"

Pinnock himself looked quite surprised at the surrounding fleet. His surprise turned to concern.

"There is no way all of these people will fit in the shuttle. I have no idea how this many people ended up here. And that's not counting you and your tribe."

"Then we have a bit of a situation here, wouldn't you agree? Would you care to speak to your High Command?" Colonus turned to the control board. "What channel?"

"Not a normal channel. It's that toggle on the far right. The small one with no label."

Colonus switched the toggle on.

"High Command, this is Major General Pinnock from community C488. Come in, please."

There was a brief pause.

"This is High Command. General, we see you have made it to Silo Six. In tow, as it appears."

"Yes sir, on both counts. I am concerned about the high number of transports here, sir. What are my orders?"

"There has been a change of plans, Pinnock. We did not anticipate such a strong and rapid response. We have decided that the shuttle will leave with only members of High Command and their families. We appreciate your dedication and service over the years, Pinnock."

There were shouts of dismay from the cabin. Pinnock motioned for Colonus to close down communication.

Pinnock was red-faced with anger. "This is total bull, Colonus! We must do something about this!"

Colonus thought a bit. "Do you think that all of High Command and their families are on the shuttle?"

Pinnock strained to see the observation screen from his seat behind the force field. "Can you pan the transports? High Command transports are larger than community transports and have a crest on the side of the protective shield. I assume from what we were told that they were not intercepted. Look for transports that have not been towed in."

Colonus moved the telescope slowly in a circle.

"There! Those four transports left center, grouped together. There must be more, though – four transports could never hold all of High Command."

Colonus peered at the screen and then turned to Pinnock. "They are probably waiting for the others. How many would you think there are?"

Pinnock paused. "There would have to be at least ten large transports, I would think."

Colonus raised his hand to near his mouth and pushed a button on the device he wore.

"This is Captain Colonus. We just got word that High Command intends to take the shuttle for themselves. The four large shuttles to the northwest of the center of the fleet with crests are High Command transports. I request that they be surrounded and not be allowed to move. I also recommend that their shells be compromised, and their transports boarded."

"Source of your information, Captain?"

"Communication between Major General Pinnock and his High Command, sir."

"Thank you, Captain."

"Sir, there may be several more High Command transports arriving soon."

Colonus turned off the observation screen.

"Latrelle, land the transport and then return to your ship and await orders."

The community transport settled onto the surface, and Latrelle opened the bay and promptly left.

Ephraim and Bailey came out when they felt the transport settle.

Colonus didn't even turn as he addressed them. "Return to your pod."

Ephraim stopped midstride and blurted, "What's going on?"

"I have no time to explain. I order you to return to your pod." Colonus turned and put an earpiece in his ear. He answered whatever he was hearing with short, curt responses.

"Yes, sir."

"No, only three."

"Two."

Colonus addressed one of his crew, "Switch to comm channel Windstorm."

Ephraim took Bailey by the elbow and took her back to the pod.

"Not good, Bales. Not good at all."

"I wonder what's happening?"

"I think we'd better do as Colonus says and wait here."

~

Outside the landscape was changing rapidly. Kiwi ships that had ferried community transports decoupled from their payloads and stood as much as at attention. Suddenly, a couple dozen headed towards the High Command transports in close formation, splitting off so two ended up positioned over each of High Command's transports, and the rest encircling them. The ships that hovered above the High Command transports lowered piercers and began breaching High Command's protective shells. Two transports were breached before several High Command defensive ships arrived. Several of the Kiwi ships that had not taken off to breach High Command raised up, reconfigured their exterior shells rapidly, and took on those attempting to protect High Command. Several more took off in search of the additional High Command transports that were expected to arrive.

The dogfight between the Kiwi and Gopher ships wasn't much more than maneuvering; neither side had strong offensive weapons. The Gopher ships attempted to grab the breaching ships with coils and pull them off the transport shells. Breaching required stability, but the Kiwis had to break breach and maneuver away to evade capture. The Kiwi ships were pestered enough that they could not stay in place long enough to breach the remaining two High Command transports. Then night came.

Colonus was the first to spot movement on the ground.

"This is Captain Colonus. The two High Command transports that were not breached have opened their hatches. There is human movement on the ground. Awaiting orders."

Pinnock's ears perked up. "Movement? Those bastards. They're going to the shuttle. Damn! They are going to take the shuttle and leave without us! Colonus, we need to go. *Now*."

Colonus scanned the observation screens. There was much movement on the ground, as people from both the Kiwis and Gophers disembarked and headed west, in long, winding queues.

"Pinnock, do you know the exact location of the Silo Six entrance? I see nothing on the screen."

"You won't see it, Colonus. The silos are ancient – left over from nuclear missiles from long, long ago. The bay doors lay flat, and the silos themselves are deep underground. I was told there would be a beacon. Do you see one?"

"No. Your communities were not very good at building batteries that could withstand the solar flares. There's nothing out there I can see. But then, the observation screen is fading... your batteries will soon be dead. The lines of people are heading due west. How many people can the shuttle hold?"

"I have no idea. I don't even know if they summoned leaders from all of the communities."

Colonus shut down the observation screen and turned around. "I doubt it can take all the people headed toward it. How did they tell you to prepare?"

"Food for three weeks and eternity pills – the entire stock after leaving enough for everyone in the community. That's all."

Colonus knocked on Ephraim and Bailey's door.

"Come on out. We have things to discuss."

Ephraim and Bailey had fallen into light sleep and walked out a little dazed. They looked around questioningly.

"It appears that people from both our tribes have broken rank and are headed on foot due west. Pinnock thinks that's where the silo is. The beacon appears to be out."

Ephraim spoke. "It's night?"

"Yes, and thankfully the night is calm. I personally don't think the shuttle can take all of the people headed out. I'm not even sure the silo bay is open."

"How long until sunrise?"

Colonus looked at his wrist piece. "Oh, maybe three hours or so. What do you want to do?"

Pinnock interrupted. "Join them! We should head out. Maybe take one of your ships to get to the head of the line. We should be first in line when the silo bay doors open."

Colonus turned to Pinnock. "Exactly how much do you know about takeoff? Time? Date? Destination?"

"I was told to arrive by 0800 hours on January 26. That's in five hours. As to destination, I have no idea. We lost communication with our pilgrim outposts many, many years ago. At least, that's what we've been told. If it were me, I'd head to the closest one. Only High Command knows where they are."

The remaining power was fading fast in the transport as Colonus turned to speak to Ephraim. Pinnock, seeing his chance and knowing the force field containing him and his crew had weakened markedly, suddenly dashed through it. He screamed in pain but did not collapse. Bradshaw and Oglethorpe followed him, wincing in pain as they ran through the force field. They bolted to the hatch door, opened it, leapt out, and sprinted toward the long line of people walking toward Silo Six's bay doors. The cool surface air blew into the transport cabin before Colonus quickly secured the hatch.

"It's going to be mayhem out there in a few hours. What do you want to do?"

Bailey hung her head. "Little chance we'll be able to fight our way on board, right?"

"We could decouple my ship and head out. I don't know where the silo access is, and there will be throngs of people fighting to get in. I imagine that High Command will get there first: they know exactly where they are going, and it's possible that they sent out a red herring for the rest to follow. That's what I would have done."

"Can you communicate with your command?"

"Yes. In my ship."

"Is there room on your ship for three?"

"Yes."

"Can we go with you, then, and see what we can learn?"

Colonus shrugged as he motioned Ephraim and Bailey to follow him. He opened up the hatch and the three of them stepped out onto the surface.

The breeze tousled Bailey's short hair. She turned to feel the wind on her face.

"Ef, I've never been on the surface. Feel that breeze!" She looked up into a clear night and saw the Milky Way strewn across the blue-black velvet sky for the first time in her life. It took her breath away.

"Ef, look up!" She twirled around, marveling at the sky. "Isn't it beautiful?"

"Come on, Bales. We need to take cover. We don't know how much radiation is in the ground. It can't be very safe for us here."

Bailey twirled again, still staring at the stars.

"Come on, Bales. Yes, it's beautiful, but we need to take cover." Ephraim gently took Bailey's elbow and headed her to the tow ship that Colonus had already reached. Colonus opened the hatch and stood back as Bailey and Ephraim boarded. He jumped in himself, secured the hatch, and went to the command panel. He busied himself flicking switches and turning dials. The panel lit up. He pushed a button and a crackle filled the cabin.

"Captain Colonus reporting in. Have you been apprised of developments?"

"Yes, Captain."

"Major General Pinnock and his crew have joined the queues headed west. I fear mayhem as they jostle for a seat on the shuttle. I have two community civilians with me. Awaiting instruction."

"Your crew?"

"I ordered them back to their ships hours ago They are en route."

"Your assessment?"

Colonus glanced at Ephraim and Bailey before starting. "There were only four High Command transports here when we arrived. I believe that it is likely that everyone gathered here from the communities was given incorrect information. There should have been several more transports here, and Pinnock was told that everyone was to be here at 0800 hours; about four hours from now. It would be my guess this silo is a ruse. It's likely that the missing High Command transports have already boarded the shuttle in a different location and will take off soon, leaving all here behind. Pinnock said he was ordered to take with him all remaining eternity pills."

There was silence on the other end. "And we were lured along with the remaining community members?"

"That would not surprise me."

"Any chance we could locate the silo and delay takeoff?"

"Doubtful."

"We will get back to you, Colonus. Stand by."

"Copy."

Colonus turned to Bailey. "You are the historian. What can you tell me about the silos?"

"There were far more than just one, but the exact number and locations were top secret. Buried in the corn fields in a places once called Kansas, Nebraska and Iowa. Far, far underground. Incredibly strong bunkers."

"Have the communities used them before?"

"Oh yes – all of our pilgrim flights left from silos. Rumor has it that there is only one missile left. Must be the one in Silo Six."

'Well, take a seat and sit tight. We have to wait for further orders." Colonus shut down all unessential equipment and slumped in his chair, taking in a quick and much-needed cat-nap. Bailey and Ephraim took seats away from the control panel and remained quiet, allowing Colonus his rest.

Dawn finally broke a few hours later. Colonus awoke to the crackle of an incoming communication.

"Captain, this is Command."

"Aye sir."

"Our ships have observed two bays opening: one to the west of you and one to the southwest. The bay directly west is only partially open and is crowded with people trying to find the foot entry point. Fights have broken out. The bay to the southwest is strangely quiet, with no apparent activity except for the fully open bay. I believe your supposition was correct. Proceed to the southwest bay to observe, but keep your distance: your mission is strictly surveillance."

"Copy that."

Colonus flicked more switches and placed his hands and feet on the controls. "Buckle yourselves in." The ship quickly but quietly rose and headed southwest. It took about fifteen minutes for Colonus to spot the open bay. He cloaked the ship to make it invisible and then maneuvered over the open bay. He hovered low, half a click northeast of the silo.

"Command, this is Captain Colonus. This silo to the southwest is apparently Silo Six. As I passed over I saw the nose of a missile. The silo registered unusual heat as we passed above it. I believe launch sequence has already commenced."

"Stand back, Captain. After launch proceed home. We will instruct our other ships likewise."

"Aye sir." Colonus muted his microphone.

"You might want to turn on your screens – there, in front of you." Colonus directed the cameras to the silo bay doors. The waves of heat rising out of the silo distorted the air unmistakably. Shortly, violent pillars of fire shot out of the bay, and the shuttle slowly raised out of the ground, rapidly gaining speed.

Bailey was both horrified and fascinated. "Ef – what are we going to do?" she said, almost whispering.

Ephraim hung his head, thinking. "Well, there certainly are no communities left for us to return to – at least, that's my guess. Even if there were, we have no idea where they are." He raised his voice a bit.

"Captain, would you consider taking us back with you to Antarctica? We have nowhere else to go."

The Captain's answer was interrupted by the crackle of a speaker.

"Captain, we just recorded a massive solar flare. You have eight minutes before it hits. Seek shelter and engage shields."

"Aye Sir." Colonus looked at the landscape around the ship – nothing but flat desert as far as the eyes could see. He flicked several more switches, and a radiation shield covered the upper hull as the ship burrowed into the dust until the ship's upper hull was level with the surrounding ground. He reached into a cubby and pulled out three sets of ear covers.

"It's going to get quite noisy very soon – here. Put these on."

In several minutes the howl of a terrible storm passed overhead, audible even through the hull, shield, and ear covers. Bailey put her hands over the earpieces and instinctively huddled down. The storm lasted no more than thirty minutes but seemed an eternity.

Colonus was taking off his ear covers when the ship was significantly rattled, accompanied by a deafening thud. Colonus engaged the camera and looked around. About a hundred yards away sat a large hunk of debris. Colonus looked skyward. He deftly lifted the ship out of the ground and headed west at a dizzying clip as thuds hit, one after another.

"What happened?" Ephraim had removed his ear protection.

"The shuttle exploded."

The cabin went silent.

"Command, this is Captain Colonus. The flare destroyed the shuttle. Awaiting instruction."

"Captain, head back northeast and surveil the dummy silo. Report back then return to base."

"Aye sir."

The ship zoomed back to the dummy silo. Colonus turned off Ephraim's and Bailey's screens as he slowly passed over the partially open bay doors. Many bodies of those that fought to get in were strewn over a large area. There was some movement within the silo, as those that had managed to enter and learn that the silo was empty had not the time to leave before the solar storm hit. The ships and transports that had been left were tossed as if they had been thrown dice on a craps table. Some were half-buried in the scorched dust and sand, and some were apparently covered entirely, resting under symmetric domes of sand.

"Significant damage to ships, Command, and heavy casualties. Some undetermined number of people survived having taken cover in the silo."

"Return to base, Colonus. We will send medical ships and transports to assist."

"Aye sir."

Colonus shifted into travel mode and the ship lurched forward as it hurled south.

CHAPTER FIVE

Colonus put his ship down on the tarmac and opened the hatch. A fresh breeze blew into the cabin and Colonus shut down all systems.

"Okay! We're here-welcome to paradise!" said Colonus with a wry grin.."

Bailey and Ephraim unbuckled and headed toward the open door. They stepped out onto the tarmac followed by Colonus, who shut the hatch and headed toward the buildings to the left. There were dozens of ships, all in a line, that stretched to their right and left. Bailey and Ephraim looked around in amazement. There were trees in the distance. There were grasses, dried brown, billowing between the tarmac and the trees. They heard the chirp of birds. Bailey gasped as she squinted in the bright sun.

"Like in the books, Ef! Green! Trees and grass!"

"Come on, Bailey. We'd better keep-up with Captain Colonus. I'm sure there will be a lot of questions and protocols we will need to get through." Ephraim shepherded Bailey, who in turn followed Colonus into a one-story, utilitarian building in the middle of a string of similar structures.

"You really do live above ground!" Bailey couldn't help but comment as the three entered the building.

"We do, but I'm not sure you can. Did you take your iodine? There's a lot more radiation here than you are equipped to handle. You need to take cover. We have some areas for people who are too sensitive to the levels of radiation topside."

Bailey and Ephraim followed the captain into the low building, where they were greeted by a small, trim woman in a pale yellow uniform. She had long, thick, curly, dark hair piled around her face.

Like Colonus, she had double-lidded eyes and thick, cinnabar-colored skin. She looked surprised to see underground folk.

Colonus spoke first. "I brought these two back from the attempted departure of the space shuttle. They are civilians who were on the High Command transport – not part of the administration. As you can see, they are Gophers."

"You'll have to excuse the Captain for calling you Gophers. That is a rather disparaging nickname our traders gave your tribe. My name is Sysiphilia."

"Ephraim Josiahson. This is my wife, Bailey."

"Welcome to Antarctica." Sysiphilia turned to Colonus. "Will these two be returning to their tribe?"

"No, that would be impossible. I will petition our leadership to allow them to stay indefinitely. Can you please set them up in temporary quarters in the sanctuary? They are not acclimated to the radiation."

"Come this way." Sysiphilia beckoned them to follow her to a door in the back of the building. "Are you hungry?"

"We are. Quite." Bailey realized they hadn't eaten since yesterday.

~

Colonus headed toward the officer's quarters. He stopped by a sentry. "Is General Bartanian available? Captain Colonus is wishing an audience."

"One moment, Captain." The sentry motioned for a second sentry to inquire in the general's office. That sentry returned shortly.

"What is the nature of your request?"

"I just returned from Silo Six and would like to brief the General."

After another brief discussion with the general, Colonus was ushered in.

"So, Colonus, am I to understand that negotiations to have some of our tribe leave on the shuttle were unsuccessful?"

"The entire shuttle was unsuccessful, General. There were many more ships and people looking to board the shuttle than there was space. A riot broke out at the silo site as people tried to find the entrance and get in. However, that silo was a decoy. A certain portion – perhaps sixty percent – of High Command went to the actual Silo Six and left the rest behind. By the time the folks at the false entrance got into the silo and realized it was empty, the crew aboard the shuttle in the actual Silo Six had fired up the rockets. However, they were rushed in their departure and were hit by a large solar storm shortly after takeoff. The shuttle was destroyed, as were most of the hapless people waiting at the decoy silo – several of our people included. They mostly perished. There might still be some alive who took shelter in the empty silo, but at the moment we simply do not know how many survived, and what shape they are in. I brought a pair of civilians from the underground back with me."

The general sat back in his chair, fingertips together in front of him, as he digested the news.

"That was the last missile?"

"We believe so, sir."

"Do you suppose that we could find the technology to build one ourselves?"

"You certainly could order a team to scour High Command headquarters and search their classified documents. But even with plans for the missile and fuel, it would take us years."

The general stared at his fingernail and absentmindedly cleaned under it with his opposing index finger.

"Do you know where the shuttle was headed?"

"The civilians mentioned that communication with the pilgrim colonies had been lost centuries ago. They thought heading for the closest known colony would have been the most obvious choice. That, though, is pure speculation."

The general sighed.

"It doesn't look good, Colonus. But we should try. I will send a team to investigate. I need to report your findings to leadership."

~

Bailey and Ephraim settled into their small compartment after eating a delicious meal with foods they had never seen: leavened bread with butter, a salad filled with fruit, nuts, and boiled eggs chopped up and garnished with butter and herbs. Their compartment was underground but somehow felt more welcoming and warmer than their former sleep pod. It had no information screen, but it did have a fairly large painting of a pastoral scene hanging on the wall – a valley with grazing creatures in the background next to a still pond with water flowers and a swan lazily swimming. There also was a small bookshelf filled with books Bailey had never seen. Bailey flopped back on the bed and placed her hands behind her head.

"I like this place, Ef. I like the people, I like the food… I like the way it feels."

Ephraim was opening doors and drawers, familiarizing himself with his new surroundings.

"Have you noticed that no one assigned us numbers or gave us our schedule?"

"Maybe it's just too early. They weren't actually expecting us, you know."

"I wonder if there are other people from different tribes here."

"I wonder how many other tribes there are!"

Bailey jumped up and started looking through the books on the shelf.

"Here's one I haven't heard about – *The Fountainhead.* Ayn Rand... I've read one of her books before. I wonder what this is about."

She started thumbing through the pages.

"You know what I would love to do? Take this book – or any book, actually – and go sit under a tree and read. Maybe by a pond, like in that picture. Just spend the afternoon sitting under a tree, reading."

Ephraim walked up behind Bailey and wrapped his arms around her waist.

"You know you can't do that, Bales. *We* can't. We don't have any resistance to the radiation."

Bailey frowned. "More of the same underground living. After seeing above ground, this is stifling."

Ephraim kissed her on her neck. "I don't want to lose you early, Bales. Hang in there for me, okay?"

Bailey tossed the book on the bed. "That's for later. Let's go explore a little. See what this place has to offer."

Bailey headed toward the door, and Ephraim followed. There seemed to be nothing but sleeping quarters underground. As they walked to the ladder that ascended to the building's above, they noticed full protective suits in a large variety of sizes hanging in a cubby near the bottom of the ladder.

"This must be how compromised people go to the surface." Ephraim held up various suits to see if there was one tall enough for him. The tallest seemed about three inches too short. The next tallest was two inches too short for Bailey. Ephraim started pulling on the bottoms of the suit he pulled out.

"Having three inches exposed is better than having no protection at all. So my waist gets irradiated. Better than nothing."

Bailey started putting on the suit Ephraim had given her. As suited up as was possible, they climbed the stairs together.

Bailey was amazed at the bustling activity in the building topside. The doors and windows were open, letting in a gentle, comfortable breeze. Men and women were bringing in goods and foodstuffs to a temporary open air market where many others were buying. Several people were wearing protective suits, and except for Ephraim's and Bailey's unusual height, no one could see that they were not of this Antarctic tribe. They walked slowly past tables brimming with all manner of items, from carrots and peas, leavened breads and cheeses to amulets, bracelets and various pieces of clothing. Bailey looked around and noticed that most people were not wearing uniforms – they were wearing flowing robes, or loose, long-sleeved shirts and billowy slacks. Some wore belts, others did not. Some had hoods, some did not. And the colors! Some were wearing blue or purple, some yellow, some green, some red. She was dumbfounded.

Bailey ambled over to a door to the outside and stopped in the threshold. Dozens of small, cinnabar-tinted people were busy getting on with their lives; going to and fro, stopping to chat with friends and acquaintances, taking shopping bags home. She stepped out into the sunlight and paused for a moment before heading out to the row of trees several hundred yards away, motioning Ephraim to follow her. She stepped onto the dried grass at the edge of the walk. The yellow-tan grass was tall, but it was brittle. Not enough rain. Bailey and Ephraim walked through it until they got to the stand of trees they had seen when they first arrived. Bailey was somewhat disappointed: these were palm trees, without broad shade. Not the broad-leafed, widely spreading deciduous trees of Bailey's book-reading fantasy. Still, they were trees. Green, living trees. Past them were fields of wilted sunflowers, heads drooping like chastised children. Even though it was dry and wilted, Bailey stood and simply gazed in wonder at the beauty of it all.

Ephraim touched Bailey's arm and motioned that they should head back. Bailey reluctantly turned and headed back with her husband.

Once back underground they removed their suits and looked at each other.

"What are we going to do now?" Bailey had already left the comfortable predictability of her former life behind. "I really want to go back outside."

"Sweetheart, you shouldn't. You are not physically prepared for that environment."

Bailey sighed. "I know." She looked longingly up the ladder and then headed back to their room. She sat on the edge of the bed, looking at the bookshelf. She picked up a book and started thumbing through it. Unable to become engaged, she put it back on the shelf. She stood and looked at Ephraim.

"I am going to suit up and go look at the market. I can't live underground all the time anymore. Look at the life up there!"

"Please, Bales…"

"You can stay here if you like." Bailey left the room.

Ephraim went with Bailey and suited up, but once on the surface he left her to wander through the rows of merchants and went to find Colonus. He was directed to a small office a few buildings away. Colonus was sitting at his desk, apparently deep in thought. Ephraim knocked.

"Yes?"

"Captain, do you have a minute?"

"Come on in, Mr. Josiahson. How can I help you?"

Ephraim grabbed a chair across from the desk and sat down.

"I noticed that the grass and sunflowers were dry and wilted. Is the weather changing here?"

Colonus stood up closed the door. He returned to his seat and looked directly at Ephraim.

"The weather has drastically changed over the past five years. We will not be able to maintain our way of life much longer. We can go underground, but it's only a matter of time before that won't work, either. At least, that's our assessment. I guess we could adopt the methods your communities used to survive for now, but our people have little appetite for that. You may have noticed that there are no young children here. About a decade ago we collectively agreed that, as we saw it, there was little future for them. We all agreed that without an alternative, we would not have children. Our last hope was the shuttle."

Colonus paused. "I have thought much about this. The underground life is not for me. It's only a matter of time before even Antarctica is uninhabitable. This planet has little to offer in the way of a future. I have never subscribed to merely surviving. I value life over survival – a good, free life. Not a life scrounging in an underground cavern."

Ephraim looked at Colonus, surprised at his candid assessment.

"You think we don't have much time?"

"I think that if I had children, by the time they are my age they would not be able to stay on the surface any longer. Our crops and livestock would be gone. I don't know whether we would be able to dig wells deep enough to find any water. This may very well could be our last generation."

Ephraim considered this.

"You can't leave for a pilgrim colony?"

"We don't have the technology. At least, not now. And I wouldn't go, anyway. I would send our youngest – that is the future. Not a wandering trader like me. No, I would give my spot for someone else. I will live and die right here."

"You are a very selfless man."

"You flatter me. No, just a realistic one."

Ephraim changed the subject.

"My wife has been hypnotized by surface life here. She is wandering the market even now. I have great concerns for her health. Hers more than mine, although I'm probably just as susceptible."

Colonus looked at Ephraim with a piercing gaze.

"Would you feel comfortable bringing children into this world, here? In Antarctica?"

Ephraim paused. "No, not really. We are not built to withstand the radiation you are adapted to."

"Would you feel content living underground among us?"

Ephraim paused.

"Honestly, not really. In our communities there were diversions and schedules that kept us occupied. We could go into a simulator and take a mountain hike, if we wanted. We could sail on open seas there. Your society doesn't have diversions like that... you live above ground."

Colonus stood up and turned around, clasping his hands behind his back.

"As my father used to say, 'you've got to die from something.' You have to ask yourself whether you want to spend your remaining days frugally-confined underground-or whether you want to spend them more quickly living a fuller life."

Ephraim sat and considered Colonus's words. He pushed his chair back and stood up. At the sound of the chair scraping the floor, Colonus turned around as Ephraim reached over, hand outstretched, to shake hands.

"You are an interesting and wise man, Captain. I will take your thoughts under consideration. Thank you so much for your time."

"Take care, Ephraim."

Ephraim sought out his wife, whom he found in front of a small stall attended by an thin, elderly woman. Bailey was admiring a pendant on a braided rope. It was a sunflower made of metal, about two inches across. The metalworker had taken great pains to make the petals and center as realistic as possible.

"This must have taken a long time to make – especially the center. It's lovely!" Bailey turned to Ephraim. "Oh, there you are. Look at this! Isn't it lovely?"

"It is." He turned to the stall attendant. "We obviously are new here and have no idea how you conduct business. Do you have a system of credits? How would I go about obtaining this for my wife?"

The wizened woman smiled kindly. "When did you arrive?"

"Today. We came with Captain Colonus."

"Ah… then you haven't yet attended orientation. You will be granted a month's worth of earnings until you get your feet on the ground." She tried to look through their protective suit's facemask. "I take it you are not well-protected from radiation on your own. If it is determined that you cannot feasibly hold a job the leaders will give you a monthly stipend. Tell you what…"

The woman gazed at the two of them. "I think I can trust you. Here – take this. When you get your stipend, you can pay me sixty divatos."

"What's your name? Are you always here, in the same spot?"

"I am. My name is Havalia."

"My name is Ephraim, and this is my wife, Bailey. Thank you for your kindness. We will be back as soon as we can be." Ephraim picked up the pendant and placed it around Bailey's neck.

"You are right. That is simply lovely." He placed his hand on her face mask, over her left cheek. "It suits you perfectly."

Bailey smiled, forgetting her face was hard to see.

"Getting hungry?"

"Yup. Let's go back down. Food is probably waiting for us."

They went back underground and took off their suits. "I like these people," said Bailey rather casually. "They seem so very… so very grown up. Trusting. Makes me want to be a better person."

"You already are a good person, Bales. You fit right in." Ephraim gave her a peck on the cheek.

Ephraim was right: there was a food tray waiting by their door. He picked it up as they entered their quarters.

"Where did you go while I was at the market?" Bailey asked between bites. Ephraim finished his biscuit before answering.

"I went to talk to Colonus. Very interesting conversation."

"Tell me more."

"Bailey, what do you want out of life?"

She was taken aback at his question.

"Well, I want beauty. And peace. I wanted kids, but now I'm not so sure. What kind of life could we offer them? It used to seem so safe and predictable. Now nothing is the same."

Ephraim paused. "I agree. I would hate to bring children into the world when the future seems so uncertain." Ephraim finished his glass of water.

"Colonus tells me that the weather has been rapidly changing. He is not sure that his people won't be driven underground, like we were. These folk have not evolved to thrive in that environment. That's why we don't see any young children here. They have collectively decided there is no future for them."

Bailey held her fork in midair at Ephraim's words.

"So Bales, what shall we do? Colonus said he'd rather spend his days more rapidly, and well, than to hoard them in what he thinks would be underground misery. All for the sake of more days."

"Like credits?"

"Yup – to him, time is just like credits. Spend them or save them."

Bailey put down her fork. "Not very hungry today," she said, placing her half-filled plate to the side. She stood up and paced a bit.

"Ef, I know this is going to be a bit hard to hear, but I think I would rather have fewer days and enjoy the wonder of the surface than to simply exist here, underground," she said, swinging her arms about the room.

Ephraim's voice was almost a whisper. "I knew you would say that." He got up and walked up behind her, wrapping his arms around her waist, leaning his head on her shoulder.

"I just knew."

"But I don't want to linger sick. That book I read back in the community? *On the Beach*? It talked about nuclear war. It spoke of radiation poisoning. When I start vomiting, getting weak and losing my hair, it will be time. I really don't want to linger. If I get sick before you do, please let me go."

"I won't want to live if you are gone, Bales." He went over to the side table and pulled out a packet. "I have eternity pills. When the time comes, we will go together."

The room hung with melancholy.

"Are you sure, Ef?"

"As sure as you are, Bales. If humans continue to exist, it's not going to be on this earth. Species go extinct. All species go extinct eventually. I think it is close to our time. No need holding on to the impossible."

Bailey spoke quietly. "Not what we had planned, huh?"

"Did we really have a plan? A life plan?"

"Not really, to be honest. Just going along with expectations. Not a lot of deep thinking going on, I guess. Funny how life can change so drastically."

Bailey fell silent for several moments. "But look at what we found! Life like we never imagined it. It's like we walked into a book.

Things I never considered before. I can't even find the words to describe the joy and wonder I felt under those trees. Even if the grass is dry – even if the sunflowers are wilted. That was worth several days of underground... maybe even several years."

She turned around so that Ephraim's arms were wrapped around her back. She smiled.

"Don't be glum, Ef. A short life of wonder and magic is better than a long life of drone and humdrum. Really. I read a poem once. '*Do not go gentle into that good night.*' Written eons ago. You and I can dance in the green bay. We can catch and sing the sun in flight. We can live, Ef. Live like we have never lived before. Relish the precious moments we have, living free and tall, breathing natural air. At this point, there's nothing else left. Is there?"

Ephraim looked at his wife in amazement. "You are a remarkable woman, Bales. So very brave. Fearless."

"Maybe just realistic, Ef. Doesn't really matter, does it?"

"Guess not."

Their discussion was cut short by a knock on the door. A younger man politely stood at the threshold.

"Mr. and Mrs. Josiahson? I am here to invite you to an orientation meeting. It will be this evening at seven, upstairs in conference room four. Once you are topside, turn right and head for the door on the far right."

"Thank you, young man."

"You are most welcome." The man turned and left. Ephraim locked the door behind him.

"You locked the door?"

Ephraim smiled. "I don't want us to be interrupted." He walked over and started removing Bailey's tunic. She smiled softly and just stood there for a moment, allowing him.

~

245

After supper Bailey and Ephraim walked into the conference room. It was small, and they were surprised they were the only orientation attendees. The room wasn't set up like a classroom or a courtroom – it was set up more like a living room, with comfortable stuffed chairs arranged across from each other with a coffee table in between. Waiting for them were an elderly couple who smiled and motioned for Ephraim and Bailey to sit down.

"Hello, and welcome to our colony! I am Polevian, and this is my wife, Theosophia. You must be Ephraim Josiahson," the man said, standing to shake Ephraim's hand. He then turned to Bailey. "And you must be his lovely wife, Bailey."

"Glad to meet you."

"Please, sit down! Can we get you anything?"

"No, we are fine, thank you." Bailey was surprised at how casual and welcoming the couple was.

Theosophia spoke up. "Dear, I see that you and your husband came up without your protective suits. We recommend you put them on every time you ascend. A bother, I know. But it's for your protection. But please also know that it is your choice."

"It's a bit difficult to remember – not what we are used to. We'll try to remember, though. Thank you for mentioning it."

Polevian assessed the two. "Very fair, you are. And very tall! I doubt you will be able to handle any more than an hour or two topside, even wearing suits. It will be difficult for you to put in a full day's work."

"Speaking of suits, the ones we found by the ladder are all too short. We put the two largest on to walk to the trees, but I had a gap of three inches around my midsection. My wife's was too short, as well – by two inches, at least."

"Well then for sure you won't be able to be topside for very long." Theosophia reached into her pocket and took out a vial. "Here.

These are iodine pills. You need to make sure you take them daily. They will give you some protection against radiation – but only some."

Bailey took the vial. "Thank you."

"I'm going to recommend that our leaders allot three months to the two of you for acclimation. Your stipend will be six hundred divatos a month. Your cavern will continue to be provided free of charge, but you will be responsible for buying everything else you need. I will investigate any jobs you may be able to perform from your quarters, but unfortunately we don't currently have any openings for remote work. If we can't find anything appropriate, the leaders will continue your stipend indefinitely."

Theosophia spoke up. "And I will see if I can get those suits of yours altered to fit." She smiled. "Do you have any questions?"

"Yes. When I went to the market I noticed fresh food. I don't know how to prepare food... I am sorry, but everything was provided for us in our community. Is there somewhere I could go to learn how to prepare food?"

Theosophia smiled. "Yes, of course. We have classes for that. I will get you a schedule. But in the meantime, why don't you come over to our place tomorrow at eleven? I will show you two how to 'emergency' eat until you get some classes under your belt."

"That is so generous of you! Where do you live?"

"Meet me here tomorrow at eleven: I will take you."

"Thank you so much!"

"Here's your first stipend. And don't forget to wear your suits."

Bailey smiled broadly. "Yes ma'am – we will."

It was still light when Ephraim and Bailey left and headed back underground. At the foot of the ladder Bailey turned to Ephraim. "Let's suit up and visit the trees again." Ef didn't hesitate – he grabbed the longest suit and started putting it on.

Topside, the hubbub of the day was gone as Ephraim and Bailey headed out through the dried grasses and over to the palm trees. Bailey grabbed a tree trunk and, leaning out, spun around it, laughing. "Let's see what's past the sunflowers."

They set off on their adventure, parting the sunflower stalks with their hands as they walked through the field. At the far edge there was a dried up river bed, and beyond was a rocky ledge. Ephraim and Bailey walked across the rocks and sand, then up onto the rocky ledge. They looked out over a steep cliff. At the bottom were piles of boulders and rocks, and past that, nearly as far as the eye could see, was white sand. Dry, barren, flat, pure white sand. Far off into the distance it seemed there was water, but it was difficult to tell, as the water could simply be horizon.

"Ef – is that water?"

"Hard to tell, Bales." Ephraim strained to see.

"I think it might be! There's a bit of movement out there – like waves. I think there is water out there! We should go see!"

"Not now, Bales. We need proper equipment to scale this wall. And that's quite some distance away… we need to plan for this."

"Are you game, then, as long as we can manage it?"

"Totally."

Bailey was elated. "Great! Let's head back and see what we can rustle up for this next big adventure."

Ephraim looked at his lovely, happy, excited wife and smiled to himself. Smiled a little sadly… he knew that the price in health for this adventure would be steep. Still, it warmed his heart to see his love so alive and in the moment. He had never seen her like this before.

The next day Ephraim managed to find some rappelling gear. It cost two hundred divatos, but Ephraim didn't care. Bailey bought a backpack and filled it with some bread, cheese and fruit from the market. Before they went to the conference room to meet up with

Theosophia, they paid the woman for the necklace they had gotten the day before. Theosophia was waiting for them, smiling, and led them to a small bungalow at the edge of the complex.

Bailey had never seen a kitchen before. She looked around – she knew what it was, from her old books, but she had no idea how anything worked.

Theosophia started with eggs.

"Eggs are easy to cook. They need to be heated. You can cook them several ways. We like scrambled." She took a few eggs, cracked them into a bowl, and stirred them with a fork.

"Just mix the clear part with the yellow until they are a uniform color. Then put them in here," she said as opened the door of an appliance. "All you need to do is push 'start.' They will come out in a few seconds, perfect. You can add cheese if you like; it will melt. Eat this with a slice of bread and that's a great small meal."

"Will this machine prepare anything?"

"Yes – it senses what you put in and does the rest of the work. Really not very complicated, unless you want to make a complicated recipe. Then you have to tell it how you want it made."

The door opened and perfectly scrambled eggs were carried out on an automated platform.

"Well, that certainly was easy." Bailey sliced some bread and spooned the eggs out onto four plates. "Let's eat."

After lunch Ephraim turned to Polevian. "We went for a walk last night, past the sunflowers on the other side of the trees. We climbed up the ledge and looked out over the sand. Tell me; was that water we saw in the distance?"

"You went that far? Yes, that's water. It used to come right to the bottom of that cliff. But over the past couple of years it has receded quite a bit. I'm pleased to hear you could still see it."

"Does anyone go out to water's edge anymore?"

"Yes – there are fishers that go to catch fish. Used to be easy. They don't bring in nearly as many as they used to. There's a deep trench, though, that's quite far from the shore. That's where what's left of the fish are. The fishers take their boats out there."

"Fascinating. How far out is the shore?"

"Oh, a mile or two. Probably more now. I haven't been there for years. We used to go, when the water was closer. Lots of people went to the beach to swim. Not anymore. The water's gotten too warm and very salty. That's why the sand is so white – it's mixed with a lot of salt."

Bailey turned to Theosophia. "What should I look for at the market between now and cooking classes?"

"You can cook any of the vegetables there – and fish. And chicken. Of course, eggs. The machine will manage those foods very well. You need to go into the communal kitchen to cook. There is one underground and one topside. The underground kitchen is small, so if it is packed you can go up the ladder. They both have machines like this. Neither have tables, though – you'll have to take your food back to your place."

"I think we can manage that. Listen, we won't take any more of your time. You have been so kind and generous. When I learn to fix food, I promise we will repay your kindness."

Theosophia just smiled. "Oh, that won't be necessary, dear."

"Thanks again." Ephraim and Bailey left.

~

The next day they headed out early, through the trees and sunflowers to the cliff.

Bailey put down the ropes she was carrying. "I bet those fishers don't scale this wall."

"You're probably right, but we have the equipment and we have no idea where they go to get to the water. Let's go... I've always wanted to rappelle down a cliff." Bailey clambered into the safety straps as Ephraim pounded in long stakes to hold the ropes.

They carefully lowered themselves to the rocks below and removed their safety straps.

Ephraim stowed the equipment at the base of the cliff and said, "Well then, my dear: first challenge met. Let's head out!" Bailey was in seventh heaven. She and Ephraim walked for several miles before they hit the water's edge. Off in the distance they could see several fishing boats bobbing gently in the rhythmic swells, their outlines muted by the mist that rose from the warm sea. Bailey took off a glove and squatted down to feel the water.

"Ouch! That's hotter than I would have guessed." She felt the sand. "The sand is cooler." "I wish these protective overalls had booties instead of being all-in-one. I would walk barefoot in the sand."

"Let's not overdo it, okay?" Ephraim took off his glove and stuck it in the surf. "Wow. That *is* warm."

They looked up and down the beach. There was nothing but sand... no seaweed, no clams, and no shells – not even fish bones. Just white, salty sand, as far as the eye could see.

Ephraim looked out again at the sea. "I wonder if we could rent a boat and go out there."

"Let's try! What a splendid idea!"

"When we get back I'll ask. But you and I should head back now."

"I guess you're right. This has been wonderful!" Bailey squeezed Ephraim's hand, and they headed back.

When they got back to their quarters there was a paper that had been slid under their door. It was the schedule of cooking classes. Bailey picked it up and read it.

"Hungry, Bales?"

"No, babe. I have no appetite at the moment. I am actually feeling a little punk. Why don't you finish the food in the backpack? I think I'll lay down for a while." She headed for the bed, laid down, and quickly fell asleep. Ephraim left and went to see if they could rent a boat.

~

Ephraim returned a few hours later to find Bailey up and vomiting. "What's wrong, babe?"

"I think I overdid it today. Let me sleep it off. We can go out again tomorrow. I'm sure I'll feel better by then." Bailey flopped back on the bed and rolled onto her side. She was asleep in no time. Ephraim went over to the side of the bed and gently stroked her hair. A patch fell out and onto her pillow. Ephraim's eyes welled up with tears.

The next morning he woke very early and headed to the market to buy eggs, cheese, fruit, and a small loaf of bread. He went to the communal kitchen to cook up some eggs with cheese. Lovely breakfast in hand, he returned to feed Bailey. She was sitting on the side of the bed when he opened the door, her hands pushing on the mattress, shoulders stooped forward, and her head hanging down.

"I brought breakfast, Bales!" He walked in, closing the door with his foot.

"I'm not hungry, hun. Go ahead and eat."

Ephraim brought her a small plate anyway. "Please try and eat, just a little. It might make you feel better."

Bailey smiled weakly and took the plate from him. She took a bite or two and then put the plate down.

"Man, I feel like I've been hit by a speeding transport."

"We did a lot yesterday, Bales. I think you should just rest today. Did you take your iodine?"

"No – forgot." Ephraim went over and got her some, returning with a little water.

"Here."

She took the iodine, laid back down, and quickly fell asleep.

Ephraim cleaned up then sat next to Bailey and held her hand while gently caressing her cheek with the back of his other hand-for hours… never leaving her side.

Bailey felt a bit better the next day. She got up and brushed her teeth. She ran a comb through her hair and a clump fell out. She hung her head.

"It's happening sooner than I thought, Ef." She nearly whispered the words.

"I know, Bales," he said. His voice was almost imperceptible.

"I don't want to feel like this."

"Go back to bed, Bales. Sleep more. You felt better this morning. Maybe you'll feel even better tomorrow."

"I hope so, Ef. This is not fun."

Ephraim picked Bailey up in his arms, cradled her, and placed her back onto the bed. "Just give it more time, Bales. Just one more day."

She sighed, kissed his hand, then rolled over and fell back to sleep.

Ephraim left Bailey and sought out Theosophia.

"My wife has radiation poisoning."

"What are the symptoms?"

"She's not hungry, was vomiting, is weak and exhausted, and some of her hair fell out."

Theosophia shook her head.

"I was afraid that would happen."

"What should I do?"

"There's not much anyone can do. Make sure she doesn't go out – she will be prone to infection. Keep her iodine up so damage to her thyroid is minimized. Hopefully she will pull through. Let me bring you your meals."

"I can't let you do that. You are too kind"

Theosophia smiled. "We all know our time here is coming to an end. The only thing we have left is kindness."

Ephraim looked at her then hugged her.

"People from the communities could have learned so much from you."

Theosophia simply smiled. She went into the kitchen and brought out some soup. "Here. I made soup this morning. Warm it up – it will be good for your wife. And for you, too."

Ephraim returned, and as he opened the door Bailey woke up.

"Feeling better? I ran into Theosophia, and she gave me some soup for you. She said she made it this morning. Give it a go? It's still warm."

Bailey smiled weakly. "I think I will." She managed several spoonsful, sitting up in bed.

"Theosophia said you overdid it. She said you need to rest for several days, and don't go out. She said she will bring meals for us. And I'm not going anywhere."

"I have radiation poisoning, Ef."

Ef hung his head. "I know, babe."

"If this doesn't get better in a week, we'll have to talk."

"Let me go try and find a library. Or a doctor. Let me read about recovery time, okay?"

Bailey sighed. "That's fair. Ef, I hate feeling this way."

Ephraim gave her a weak, pained smile. "I know, babe. I wish it was me instead."

"Trust me, you don't." She laid back down with a sigh. "Tell Theosophia that her soup was delicious."

The following day Ephraim returned with a doctor. He examined her and asked where she had been and what she had done.

"I'm no expert on your biology. I have been treating our people my whole life. That being said, it's obvious that you have been exposed to far too many rads. Not enough to kill you immediately, but enough that you should have no further exposure for a couple of years. None! Not even while suited up in protective gear. You should regain your appetite in a week or two. You will most likely lose the rest of your hair, but it will grow back, and your strength will slowly return."

Bailey looked bleakly at Ephraim. "Thank you, doctor."

The doctor turned to Ephraim. "If she gets an infection you must get her on antibiotics. Any worsening in condition, call me."

"Thank you, doctor." Ephraim closed the door after the doctor and went to Bailey's side.

Bailey looked at him. Her voice was resolute. "Ephraim, I will not live underground for the next two years."

Ephraim looked at her, his eyes flitting back and forth as he focused on one eye, and then the other.

"But Bales, you'll get better if you follow the doctor's orders."

"I can get better, but can I enjoy life? Do I need to pay for half a day of joy with two years of confinement? Here?" She waved her arm, motioning the quarters around them. "What's left for us?"

Ephraim looked down at his hands.

"What do you want to do, Bales?"

Bailey sat in silence for a few minutes.

"You know what I want? I want to watch a sunrise. I have never watched the sunrise. We go to the edge of the trees and sit under one, and watch the sun rise over the sunflowers. Wouldn't that be lovely?"

Tears ran down Ephraim's face. Bailey choked up, and tears ran down her face, too.

"Please, Ephraim? Can we go watch the sunrise?"

Ephraim replied woodenly. "When, babe?"

"I think maybe tomorrow. Tomorrow would be a lovely day to watch a sunrise."

Ephraim swallowed.

"Ef, I don't want you to get sick like me. I don't want us living here, like this. Let's do what we agreed to do. Let's catch and sing the sun in flight."

Ef kissed his wife and the salt from their tears mingled and stung their lips.

Early the next morning, Ephraim and Bailey walked up the ladder, unencumbered by protective suits. They slowly walked, hand in hand, in the pre-dawn light to the far edge of the trees and settled in against the trunk of the largest tree at the edge of the stand of trees, facing the sunflower field. Very soon, on the horizon, over the wilted sunflowers, the sky began glowing in the palest of yellows. It then warmed with a rosy glow, and then shafts of light hit some drifting clouds, transforming them into fiery orange and purple opals. The sky beneath these clouds glowed in an even brighter orange, yellow, and red, until the burning orb slowly lifted its heavy weight and ascended over the wilted sunflowers. Fiery and huge, it commanded the sea and sand beneath it in its terrifying glory, turning both sand and sea scarlet red. The sun lumbered higher still, lifting itself, inexorably, into the sky above. And as it rose, the colors surrounding it faded in the bright wake of its commanding and fierce red fury, until no longer partially hidden by the sunflowers, it faded the colors around it to blue and white... until it, itself, faded to yellow.

"Isn't it beautiful? Wasn't that sunrise spectacular?" Bailey turned to Ephraim, leaned over and kissed him sweetly... kissed him warmly,,, then kissed him deeply. "I love you, Ef. It's been grand with you, you know? Simply grand. I can't imagine anyone better than you."

"I love you too, Bales. To the moon and back."

"To the moon and back."

They laid down under the arching branches of the palm tree and snuggled in. They then placed an eternity pill onto each other's tongues and looked deeply, one last time, into each other's eyes. And then they kissed again. The kiss was long and deep, lasting until they fell contentedly into eternal sleep, holding each other tightly as the sun rose ever higher and ever brighter into the blazing sky above.

WENDY SURA THOMSON

ABOUT THE AUTHORS

Andrew Charles Lark graduated from Wayne State University, receiving his Bachelor of Arts degree in English. His play, *Stop Up Your Ears!,* a farcical month in the life of Florence Foster Jenkins, won Wayne State University's Heck-Rabi award and was produced at the Hillberry Studio Theatre in Detroit, Michigan. His play, *The Embrace of Redemption,* received several readings, and *Ask Me! Tell Me!,* was professionally produced at both Ringwald Theatre's GPS in Ferndale, Michigan, and also the Hudson Theatre's Play by Play Festival in Hudson, New York, where it won a Ten Best award. *Better Boxed and Forgotten* is his first novel. Andrew is currently working on his second novel, *The Persistence of Whispers,* and a children's illustrated book titled *Monstergarten.* Andrew is the writer and director of the upcoming podcast series, *Dark Waters,* which will be available on Sound Cloud soon. His other works, announcements, and musings can be accessed at www.alarksperch.com. He lives in St. Clair Shores, Michigan, with his wife Karen, and Georgie the corgi-terrier mix who strikes fear in the hearts of all neighborhood rabbits and squirrels.

Donald Levin is an award-winning fiction writer and poet. He is the author of six novels in the Martin Preuss mystery series, as well as a mainstream novel, *The House of Grins*, and two books of poetry, *In Praise of Old Photographs* and *New Year's Tangerine*. He lives in Ferndale, Michigan. To learn more about him and his work, please visit www.donaldlevin.com and follow him on Twitter at @donald_levin, Facebook at Donald Levin, Author, and Instagram at donald_levin_author.

Wendy Sura Thomson is a five-star author with two previously published works: *Summon the Tiger* (2016) and *The Third Order* (2018.) She has two additional titles in the works: *The Man from Burntisland* and *Ted and Ned*. She finds herself incredibly busy for someone who ostensibly retired several years ago, still freelancing in the financial arena for a few clients, as well as her writing, painting, and gardening. She lives in Bloomfield Hills, Michigan, with her two Irish Setters, Riley and Shiloh. Visit her at www.quittandquinn.com, follow her on Twitter @1amwendy, follow her on Facebook at Wendy Thomson, and on Instagram at wsurathomson.

Other Books by the Authors

Andrew Charles Lark

Better Boxed and Forgotten (The Archive Series, volume 1.) A horror/suspense novel about what happens when a man inherits the family mansion and discovers his great-grandfather's meticulously archived treasure trove of lost papers, secret military hardware, and fantastic inventions – and one invention in particular, whose strange and fantastic powers inadvertently open doors with fatal and deadly consequences.

Donald Levin

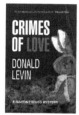

Crimes of Love. When a seven-year-old girl goes missing off the streets of his suburban Detroit city, police detective Martin Preuss probes deep into the anguished lives of her family for the awful secret to her disappearance in the first novel of this mystery series.

The Baker's Men. A fatal shooting at a local bakery draws Martin Preuss into a whirlwind of greed, violence, and revenge that spans generations across Metropolitan Detroit.

Guilt in Hiding. When a minibus belonging to a group home for handicapped adults disappears, Martin Preuss's search exposes a multitude of crimes with roots in the twentieth century's darkest period.

The Forgotten Child. A friend asks Martin Preuss to look for a boy who disappeared forty years ago, and his investigation takes him back to the countercultural fervor of Detroit in the 1970s and plunges him into hidden worlds of guilty secrets and dark crimes that won't stay buried.

Other Books by the Authors

Donald Levin

An Uncertain Accomplice. Now a private investigator, Martin Preuss is hired to track down a previously-unknown accomplice to a kidnapping/murder, a case that entangles him in a web of deceit stretching across Metropolitan Detroit from the mega-rich suburbs to a hardscrabble trailer park.

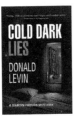

Cold Dark Lies. Martin Preuss sets out to discover how a young man wound up clinging to life in a disreputable Ferndale motel, but quickly discovers nothing is as it seems in the young man's world of secrets and lies.

Wendy Sura Thomson

Summon the Tiger. A memoir of a resilient and indefatigable woman who finds success against all odds.

The Third Order. A suspenseful novel of a young woman whose accidental possession of a strange, ancient artifact leads her on a cross-continent search for its meaning – and why a secretive, rogue religious group is in hot pursuit.

Made in the
USA
Monee, IL